GALLEON

A Novel By
Mark Moorer

Published by Little Studio Films

ISBN: 979-8-9919433-5-2
LCCN: 2025911185

Edited by: Heidi Stangeland
Cover by: Mark Moorer

For Meme, Mom, Dad, Marianne, Kristin,

Jessica, Riley, Jace, Alec, Trey, and A.J.

With God, all things are possible.

GALLEON has been a journey—one that started years ago as a screenplay and refused to stay confined to the screen. The characters, the world, and the story kept calling me back, asking to be explored more deeply, to live and breathe beyond the edges of a script.

Writing this novel allowed me to revisit the story with fresh eyes and a fuller heart. It's a tale of adventure, mystery, and transformation—but at its core, it's about the pull of destiny and the choices we make when we're faced with the unknown.

To those who've supported me in bringing *GALLEON* to life—my family, friends, and creative collaborators—I'm overcome with gratitude. Your belief in this story made it possible for me to tell it in a new and unexpected way.

Thank you for coming aboard.

Contents

The Arabelle

On the stormy night of November 13th, 1632, the Arabelle—a majestic galleon stretching 150 feet—succumbed to the fury of the Atlantic. Time and tide clashed in a hurricane's wrath off the coast of Florida. The wind howled like a banshee, its wail a tangible force that clawed at the ears of an exhausted crew, threatening to tear them from their crumbling vessel.

Waves surged like liquid mountains, ancient and enraged. Blinding salt spray burned their eyes as a monstrous wall of water engulfed the ship. For an instant, it revealed the Arabelle's battered elegance—her once-proud sails now tattered flags in the storm's relentless grip. Rain, cold and merciless, flayed their skin in sheets of icy blades.

A twenty-foot breaker slammed into the bow, drowning men in a flash-flooded tomb. The ship groaned, rose, heaved—and then another wave hit, larger, angrier. A deafening roar and a cataclysmic crash tore the breath from their lungs. Agonized screams, strangled and primal, were swallowed by the storm's monstrous voice. Six men—faces twisted in pain—were yanked into the abyss, consumed whole by the sea's insatiable maw.

A desperate handful remained. Clinging to splintered masts and frayed rigging, they fought a losing battle against nature's wrath. The Arabelle moaned like a dying beast, her timbers buckling under pressure no ship could withstand. Each sickening pop was a wooden dowel torn free—each a drumbeat in the dirge of disintegration. Then came the splitting crack as the deck cleaved, followed by the soul-splintering snap of the mainmast's fall.

Miguel, the boatswain's mate, his eyes wide in silent terror, stood frozen as the mast came down. It crushed him instantly—a grotesque punctuation to the chaos. Another wave, vast and vengeful, WHOOSHED across the deck, extinguishing the last human cries.

Alone now, hands bleeding and raw, one man clung to the battered starboard railing. Twenty-three years at sea—sun-drenched ports, whispered songs, star-strewn nights—all of it distilled into this single, brutal hour. A night pitched against oblivion.

The *Arabelle* was dying.

Water surged through a jagged rupture in her deck, cascading into her belly with the inevitability of fate. The sea, relentless and swollen with rage, poured in like a predator sensing blood. A single backward glance revealed the stern already slipping beneath the waves—slowly, silently, as if trying to hide its shame.

At the helm, the captain stood rigid, knuckles pale against the rain-slicked mahogany wheel. His grip, though fierce, was beginning to fail. In his other hand, clutched tight against his chest, was a rough burlap sack—its shape obscured by the storm, its importance betrayed only by the way he held it, as though it contained the memory of an entire world. Salt stung his eyes. Not tears. Not yet.

"Captain!" Carlos's voice cracked through the wind, high and ragged. "What do you want me to do?" The storm offered no answer. It bellowed and churned, deaf to mortal pleas. A wave rose— twenty feet high, maybe more—and collapsed over the bow with a roar that drowned even thought. Water thundered across the deck, cold and solid as a falling wall, carrying away ropes, barrels, and men alike. Somewhere within the ship's frame, the timbers split with a sickening crack. The *Arabelle* groaned, her bones breaking under the weight of the ocean's fury.

The captain turned. His eyes were wild now— haunted, but sharp with purpose. He stepped forward and thrust the sack into Carlos's chest. The young man recoiled slightly at the scratch of the fabric, rough and soaked, before instinct took over and he gripped it.
"You must survive," the captain said. His voice was low, forced through the grind of wind and rain. "You must carry this. Make sure we are not forgotten."
Carlos stared at him, stunned into silence. The man before him looked like a stranger—face weathered and worn by decades of wind, salt, and guilt—yet in that moment, he felt like something - closer. Not quite a father.
Not quite a ghost. But something in between. A heartbeat passed. Then another.

Carlos reached beneath his sodden shirt, fingers

fumbling in the cold, and drew out a gold cross. The emeralds embedded in it caught what little light remained, gleaming like eyes in the dark. It pulsed with heat despite the chill, as if it remembered everything that had come before—before-the prayers whispered into it, the blood it had watched spill, the storms it had already survived.

Without thinking, Carlos tore it from his neck. The chain snapped. He pressed the cross into the captain's hand.
The older man nodded once, solemn and sharp. His expression was unreadable—part grief, part fire— but it held no doubt. He didn't look back. He didn't hesitate.
"Go," he said. Not a shout. Just a command. Quiet. Final.
And then the sea rose again.
The captain's voice rang out—raw, urgent, unyielding. A final command from the heart of the storm.

Carlos stumbled across the slick, splintering deck, no more than a ragdoll hurled by the furious wind. A wooden hatch cover tore loose and swung toward him like a pendulum of death. He dropped to the boards just in time, the heavy slab crashing into the hull behind him with a sickening thud—an executioner's hammer swallowed by the groaning timbers of the dying ship.

Scrambling to the port side, he found himself face to face with a churning vortex where the sea gnawed at the ship's shattered belly, a monstrous mouth widening with every heartbeat. He turned—just for a moment—and saw the captain. A fleeting glimpse, but it branded itself onto his soul.

The old man stood still against the chaos, a shadow against the black, clutching the gold cross to his chest. His face was carved with a final, unflinching truth. Their eyes met, and the captain gave a small, almost imperceptible nod.

One last farewell.

Carlos seized the hatch with shaking hands, driven by a strength summoned from the deepest corners of fear. With a desperate cry, he hurled it into the storm. Then he clutched the burlap sack to his chest—its weight unfamiliar, impossibly heavy—and stepped to the edge.

A scream tore from him. Not a cry for help, but a sound older than language—a howl of grief, rage, and hope. It ripped through the wind as he threw himself into the sea.

Behind him, the *Arabelle* reared back, her bow jutting into the air like the skeletal finger of a dying god, pointing toward the abyss. Salt spray stung the captain's face, sharp and cold as broken glass. His

hands still gripped the wheel, though the wheel no longer answered him. With a voice hoarse from salt and sorrow, he bellowed one final roar into the storm—a cry of defiance hurled at the heavens.

Before him, the Atlantic opened like a wound, a cauldron of black, roiling water. The air thickened with the stench of brine and something darker—death, old and patient. And then, with a sound like the sky itself being torn, the ocean swallowed the *Arabelle* whole.

But the sea, it seemed, had other plans.

The ship convulsed in its final death throes—a frantic, futile dance—before plunging into the smothering dark. The ocean swallowed it whole, dragging down the screams of the dying until nothing remained but the wind and the crash of waves against the shore.
Dawn seeped across the sky in hues of ash and decay, bleeding a sickly grey over the ravaged horizon. Rain fell in cold, relentless sheets, a frigid curtain that lashed the coastline.
Each wave struck the sand like a hammer, reshaping the world with every blow. Carlos's mouth filled with salt and blood as a monstrous swell hurled him ashore, tossing his body across the beach like wreckage. He lay still, a broken shell emptied by the sea.

Gasping, he clung to the shattered hatch cover—more driftwood than shield now—as if it might still save him. His fingers, numb and raw, refused to loosen their grip on the sodden burlap sack. He held it close, as if it contained not only his last hope, but the final piece of himself.

A fragile tether to life in the face of annihilation. With a groan, he rolled onto his side and pulled the sack from the crook of his arm. Rain sluiced across its surface, revealing a gleam of brass beneath the grime. The outline of the *Arabelle*'s bell emerged— smooth, solid, and cold—its inscription barely legible, a name carved into metal now turned memorial. The cursed *Arabelle*, her legacy etched in the iron echo of silence.

The bell, heavy with seawater and grief, sank into the wet sand. Even motionless, it seemed to vibrate with loss, a silent testament to the wreckage and all it had consumed. Beside it, the ragged sack slumped open, the contents obscured.

Carlos stared at it, the storm still clawing at his skin, the wind still howling like the dead. Whatever lay within might redeem him or destroy him. He did not know. But in the marrow of his bones, where instinct whispered what reason dared not, he felt it:

Some things should never return from the deep.

Arabelle, 1632

Treese

The lifeboat pitched violently, a fragile cradle tossed between two monstrous shadows. On one side, the *Sea Wench* loomed—a seventy-five-foot commercial fishing vessel gleaming malevolently beneath a bruised moon. On the other side, the hulking freighter sat heavy and rusted, its corroded planks scarred by years of unforgiving seas.

The air hung thick with the coppery tang of blood and the acrid sting of salt spray. Twelve figures cloaked in camouflage moved like ghosts, their faces masked and unreadable. They herded ten terrified Hispanic men—faces etched with fear, eyes wide with the grim understanding of their fate—down a rope ladder that swayed like a hangman's noose.

The last man, a young buck with a sleeve ripped away to reveal a crimson river tracing his arm, tumbled into the lifeboat, a desperate gasp escaping his lips.

Davis, the camo-clad leader, stood at the freighter's railing like a predator. Wiry and deceptively slight, his thirty-five years belied a coiled strength ready to snap. His pale, calculating eyes swept over the huddled men. With a practiced, almost contemptuous flick of his wrist, he hurled four water jugs into the boat—meager sustenance against the vast, indifferent ocean—followed by a small, ominous device: the beacon.

His voice broke through the night like a low growl,

thick with the drawl of the backwoods South. "That beacon activates in twenty-four hours. Y'all be good now," he spat, the menace in his words lingering like a dark cloud.

The threat hung heavier than the humid air.

Behind them, the freighter's lights faded, swallowed by the inky blackness. The men were left adrift in a sea of despair.

The distant engines of the *Sea Wench* pulsed like a malevolent heartbeat, mocking their helplessness. Ten souls abandoned, cast into the void. The bitter taste of betrayal clung to their tongues, the cold certainty of death their only companion in the vast, uncaring dark.

The desperate hope flickering in their eyes was snuffed out swiftly, drowned beneath overwhelming despair and the chilling premonition of the merciless hours ahead.

Salt spray stung Romer Treese's face as he yanked the camouflage mask down from his jaw, the rough fabric scraping against skin already tight with anticipation. His crew cut—bleached almost white by relentless sun—caught the harsh dawn light, shining like a beacon of hardened resolve. This wasn't some Navy SEAL exercise. This was real. The culmination of months of navigating a labyrinth of deceit and blood money.

He moved with the predatory grace of a seasoned killer. The deck groaned faintly beneath his boots as he stalked toward the metal containers.

Davis, his face carved with a mixture of apprehension and grim satisfaction, followed close behind, along with the other camo-clad men whose eyes burned with feverish excitement. The engine thrummed beneath them, a deep, guttural growl vibrating through the hull—a relentless pulse echoing the frantic beat of Treese's own heart.

East, toward Plana Cay—the promised land. Four hundred hours. Their rendezvous with fate.

The hiss of Treese's hydraulic cutter sliced the thick air, a metallic shriek matching the tension coiled tight in his gut. He heaved open the first box. The stench of ozone and high explosives filled his nostrils.

Two Stinger missiles—sleek and deadly—rested within their launcher, gleaming malevolently in the weak dawn light.

Treese's smile was slow and predatory, the curl of his lips a stark contrast to the cold, calculating glint in his eyes. This wasn't just a weapons deal. They weren't unloading cargo—they were selling their souls. The entire bloody ship.

A collective gasp, barely stifled, slipped from Davis and the others. Surprise clashed with brutal, exhilarating greed in their eyes.

The ship—their ticket to oblivion or unimaginable wealth.

Tonight, the choice was theirs to make.

The LaPointe Legacy

St. Augustine, Florida. Rain lashed the ORCA, a research vessel more accustomed to sun-drenched Caribbean waters than this brutal Atlantic squall. The wind howled a mournful dirge—a fitting soundtrack for the mission ahead.

Inside Jack LaPointe's quarters, cramped and smelling faintly of stale beer and ambition, an electric guitar amp stood battered and scarred like its owner. Jack, a man forged from restless energy and shadowed by the legacy of a legendary father, shredded a blistering solo. His dark hair clung to his forehead, a three-day beard framing a jaw clenched in fierce concentration. A whirlwind of raw talent, he was a scientist who had traded his lab coat for a leather jacket.

The chaotic notes he scribbled on a crumpled sheet of music matched the tempest raging outside. Suddenly, his phone buzzed—a jarring interruption. NEED YOU ON DECK.

The message, curt and ominous, wiped the defiant grin from his face. He slammed the guitar down, silence amplifying the storm's fury.

Exiting the hatch, Jack battled the wind, his movements precise and economical like a seasoned deep-sea diver.

At the bow, Chip Johnson, his research assistant—a skinny kid with the nervous energy of a caffeinated squirrel—scanned the churning ocean through binoculars.

"Not to be a nudge, Jack, but I still think this is a monumentally bad idea," Chip called out, his voice barely audible over the roaring wind.

"It wouldn't be my first," Jack replied, weariness threading his tone.

"You're good," Chip said, "though I doubt he even knows your name."

"Last time I checked, his signature was on my paycheck," Chip shot back, undeterred.

"If I had a vote…" Jack began.

Chip whipped out his iPhone, "Gotta document this. Insta-famous, here we come! I set up an Instagram for The ORCA."

"What did I say about that social media crap?" Jack growled.

"We're real influencers, Jack!" Chip insisted. "The follower fanbase alone—"

Greg Sandoval, the ORCA's new pilot, interrupted. Miami-bred, tanned skin pulled tight against the wind, Greg's Spanish-inflected English crackled with urgency.

"Got the update, bro. Category Two hurricane brewing between Jacksonville and St. Augustine. Four hours tops. Pero, like, it's now or never."

Jack's grim smile deepened. "Then let's crank her up."

Greg nodded and sprinted toward the bridge.

As the ORCA sliced through mountainous waves, a defiant blast of rock music—rebellion and defiance—ripped from the deck speakers.

The storm raged outside, mirroring the turmoil churning inside Jack LaPointe's soul.
The hunt was on.

The rusty bulkhead door groaned open, and Jack stepped through, his face etched with a weariness born from a lifetime spent dodging rogue waves—and even more roguish men. The cramped control room felt like the guts of a submarine after a kraken attack: a chaotic symphony of blinking lights and whirring hard drives.
Monitors, a dazzling array of screens vying for attention, stretched across the opposite wall, culminating in a monstrous big-screen behemoth. Jack moved with the practiced grace of a seasoned deep-sea diver—his motions economical, his eyes sharp and calculating like a shark's.
A few brutal mouse clicks brought the big screen to life, revealing the research vessel Albatross—a sleek, white giant cutting through the digital waves.

They battled a churning sea the color of bruised plums. Two technicians sat pale-faced beneath the harsh glare of flickering monitors in the cramped control room. The video call crackled to life.
"Albatross, this is Orca. What's the damage, guys?" Jack's voice, gravelly from years shouting over tempestuous seas—and even more tempestuous arguments—boomed across the room.
A wiry technician, barely out of his twenties, leaned into the camera, eyes wide with a mix of apprehension and excitement.

"Hey, Jack. You made it! You outrun that squall?"
"In progress. Where's the old man?" Jack's tone sharpened, steel threading through his words.
The technician glanced nervously left, then backpedaled quickly. From the shadows emerged Dr. Will LaPointe—sixty years carried lightly, a silver fox with piercing blue eyes beneath a black baseball cap emblazoned with the Albatross's crest. A legend, a modern Jacques Cousteau, whose televised adventures masked a deep sorrow, he drowned in relentless scientific pursuit.
"Hello, son," Will said calmly, weariness lining his voice like Jack's own.
"Dad."
"I'm busy, Jack. What is it?"
"We finished the methane scan at the Outer Ridge. Heading south to outrun this storm. Thought we'd swing by."
Will subtly gestured at the technicians, who vanished with practiced alacrity, slamming the hatch shut behind them with a metallic clang that echoed the tension.
Will turned back to the screen, face unreadable.
"No."
"For Christ's sake, Dad! Why are you locking me out?" Jack's voice was a low growl.
Will offered only a blank stare.
"You know I want to be more involved in the shows. Let me help you."
Will's eyes narrowed. "You are helping. Since 2012, methane hydrate beds along the East Coast have exploded, from three to nearly six hundred. Every

new document strengthens my theory.”
His fingers tapped furiously at the keyboard, precise and economical.
“Remember my trip to the Arctic Circle last year?”
A chill ran down Jack's spine.
“So… this is about the polar bears?”
“Not just the polar bears.”
A second monitor flickered to life, revealing footage that sent a shiver through Jack.
A brutal Arctic wind whipped around Will, his parka billowing as he stood on the icebreaker's bow.
Towering ice floes churned in a sea the color of steel.
A solitary polar bear balanced precariously on a shrinking iceberg—a stark symbol of looming catastrophe.
Both polar ice caps were melting. The Arctic was warming faster than anywhere else on Earth.
Evidence pointed to a hidden super volcano beneath it all.

The camera cut to the Arctic seabed, revealing an immense miles-wide caldera—a simmering volcanic giant spewing plumes of superheated methane gas and chunks of ice into the frigid waters.
Methane bubbles erupted at the surface as small ice floes sank beneath the waves. The Arctic Ocean— half a world of ice—was rapidly losing its icy grip.
A Google Earth shot revealed the horrifying truth: a half-blue, half-white expanse, the white shrinking alarmingly.
“A caldera bigger than Yellowstone… spewing superheated methane into the Arctic Ocean…” Jack

whispered, eyes wide with dawning horror.

Raising ocean temperatures around the globe — an unholy inferno burning beneath the waves — was frying sea life faster than a deep-fried clam at a Coney Island cookout. Polar ice caps melted like popsicles left out in the blazing heat of a July Fourth parade. And methane, that insidious, invisible killer, trapped heat twenty times worse than CO_2 — a planet-sized pressure cooker ticking ominously. Fifteen to twenty years? Arctic ice? Gone. Kaput. Finished. Like a cheap tequila sunrise fading fast. Massive Antarctic waves, the kind that could swallow a destroyer whole, slammed relentlessly against the base of ice mountains the size of small countries. Then came the sound — a planet cracking, shattering the silence — crack!

A chunk of ice larger than an aircraft carrier broke free with a thunderous roar that shook the very bones of the Earth.

And then, a thirty-foot tsunami, a monstrous wall of white fury, surged forward, an unstoppable force born from the collapse of the frozen giants.

The capped fury surged outward — a liquid death sentence unleashed. And that was only the beginning. Vast swaths of Antarctic ice shelves, colossal enough to make Manhattan look like a grain of sand, teetered on the brink of collapse.

This wasn't just climate change; this was a global climate apocalypse. A tipping point. A domino effect. A runaway train barreling toward the edge of a cliff. Rising seas would drown coastal cities by 2050, swallowing them whole.

And in the worst-case scenario? Our kids would face
an extinction-level event — a grim rerun of the
dinosaur snuff film, only this time, *we* were the stars.
The tsunami image froze on the screen. Will's face,
worn by a thousand sleepless nights, turned to his
son, Jack.

"We're calling it 'The Extinction Protocol,'" Will said,
voice tight with urgency.

"Seriously? Isn't that a bit dramatic?" Jack shot back,
skepticism barely hidden.

"That's why you're not running the show, son," Will
snapped, eyes icy. "Follow orders, or I'll take back
The Orca."

"The Orca is my ship!"

Will leaned back, exasperated. "No, Jack. It's my ship.
And the only reason you're still captain is because
you're my son. The investors... they don't have the
stomach for..." His voice faltered, gaze drifting away.

"For a fresh take!?" Jack pressed.

The pain cracked through Will's steely façade — raw
and unmistakable.

"I don't have time for micromanagement. Just ride
out the storm and get me that report."

Will jabbed at the mouse. The monitor went black.
Jack stared at the blank screen, disgust twisting his
features. He shoved away from the console and
stormed out.

Jack slammed his finger onto the sonar screen, the
glowing image searing itself into his mind. "Methane
hydrate. I'm going down."

A feral grin cracked across Chip's face, knuckles
white as he shadow-boxed the air. "Finally," he

growled, a guttural rasp against the howl of the wind. "Some action."

The Orca groaned beneath the tempest, a living beast battered by icy claws scraping her hull. Salt spray stung Jack's eyes as he lunged for the railing—taut, muscular, clad in a wetsuit, fins slung over his shoulder. The cold metal of his AGA full-face mask pressed against his fevered heartbeat.
Bobbi and Sam, two crew members chiseled by the Australian sun, moved with the fluid grace of sharks—crew cuts plastered to their skulls, concern etched on faces usually carved by the unforgiving sea. They wrestled tanks and gear with surgical precision, a deadly ballet of preparation. Chip, a whirlwind of restless energy, shoved a tarp-covered object toward them, breath ragged in the gale.
Then, a monstrous wave slammed into the Orca's side—a liquid hammer blow—sending icy sheets cascading over the deck. Bobbi ripped away the tarp, revealing "Rover," a compact three-by-three-foot ROV, its black box video camera a malevolent eye staring coldly from the deluge.
Greg's voice, raw with fear and urgency, cut through the storm's roar. "Jack, you're crazy! You wanna rethink this? There's a whole squadron of squalls closing in behind us!"
Jack's gaze, steely and unyielding, locked with Greg's. "Ten minutes," he rasped, the wind snatching the words before they could fully form.
The air hung thick with ozone and salt, mingling with the metallic tang of fear.

He and Sam fought into their gear, brutal and swift. Chip and Bobbi, muscles straining, lowered Rover into the churning Atlantic. Jack vaulted onto the dive platform, the impact jarring as a monstrous wave slammed into the hull, then plunged into the frigid ocean's icy grip. Sam followed, a silent prayer flickering in his eyes.

Below, Bobbi's fingers—numb and trembling—scrubbed the waterproof iPad's screen as the silt-choked image of Jack and Sam flickered, ghostly figures trapped in a watery tomb.
The images blurred, the comms crackled and fractured. The cold clawed at Jack and Sam as they battled the current, fighting to hold their course. Rover, their mechanical sentinel, cast a pale, wavering glow ahead.
Sam's voice, a grim whisper barely piercing the storm, broke the tension. "Couldn't we have just used the new Rover, Jack?" His tone carried fear — and something else: a grudging respect for Jack's reckless resolve.
Jack's response was a guttural laugh, half-drowned by the tempest. "If it's a methane hydrate bed this far south... I want to see it. Myself."

The seafloor loomed—dark, mysterious. Rover pushed onward, its lights slicing through the gloom, revealing a breathtaking scene of eerie beauty and terrifying promise.
Chip's voice crackled over the comms, static slicing through the chaos. "Methane output... minimal..."

Sam's eyes rolled, a storm of awe and disgust swirling within. "'I just wanted to see it for myself.' What a piece of work, man," he muttered, the words swallowed by the vast, unforgiving ocean. Around them, the air seemed to hum with silent understanding — they faced something ancient, immense, deadly. And Jack, reckless to the core, was dead set on staring into its abyss.

A vortex of churning sand and water tore at them. The roar was deafening, a physical blow to their eardrums. The current—an invisible, monstrous hand—clawed at Rover, yanking it backward with savage force. Jack tasted grit, the metallic tang of fear coating his tongue. Sam's strangled gasp was swallowed by the wind's howl. Their fingers, raw and bleeding, dug into the crumbling cliff, coarse rock biting into flesh.

"Hang on!" Jack screamed, his voice a fragile thread lost in the swirling chaos.

"What the hell?" Sam gasped. The Rover bucked like a wild beast fighting for its life, headlights slicing through the roiling murk. Then—a fleeting shadow. A monstrous shape rising from the sand as if birthed from the abyss itself. A galleon.

The Rover—metal coffin—was snatched away, swallowed by ravenous depths. Total, suffocating blackness, pierced only by frantic beams from their helmet lamps. Chip's panicked voice, a desperate crackle on the comm, barely broke through the static roar. The current, a relentless hungry beast, sucked sand and debris into the ravine's gaping maw—a

grinding symphony of destruction.
Jack and Sam exchanged a look heavy with shared terror, a silent pact forged in the jaws of death.
Then, as suddenly as it began, the current eased. The grip loosened.
"Whoa," Jack breathed, voice raw, body trembling. "You okay, Sam?"
Sam let out a choked laugh, more reflex than answer. "Is that a joke? Are you kidding me?"
"Jack! Jack! Do you copy? Jack, you there, man?!" Chip's frantic voice crackled through the comm.
"Yeah, yeah," Jack rasped, words tasting like ash. "We're okay... but we lost the Rover."
They scanned the silt-choked water, disoriented, bodies screaming in protest. Then—a flicker of hope. A metal shape rising from the depths.
"Hang on, hang on... Nope, there it is! I got him!" Sam shouted, triumph cutting through exhaustion.
The Rover surfaced, coughing up water and sand.
"Good. Let's get out of here."
As it pulled away, a dim light caught Jack's eye—a shape on the ridge, half-buried, half-revealed.
"What in the blue hell is that?" Jack gasped, kicking off toward the ridge, adrenaline overruling the fear.
Sam grimaced. "Really? Now?"

But as they drew closer, their gasps turned from protest to wonder. No words could capture the sight. The galleon. ¨Immense, majestic, utterly wrecked. Its hull leaned precariously, a gaping hole torn in the deck. The main mast lay splintered, the bow buried deep in sand.

Late afternoon sun pierced a break in the clouds, casting long shadows that stretched like ghosts across the scene, highlighting the sheer scale of the find. A Spanish galleon, lost to time, its secrets swallowed by the relentless sea.

Hours later in the Mid-Atlantic, the ORCA—a research vessel that looked like it had weathered a dozen hurricanes without losing an ounce of bite—sliced through mountainous seas with the ferocity of a killer whale avoiding capture.
Apt name. Rain lashed the decks, a stinging curtain blurring the fading light.

Inside, the lab buzzed like a hive—beeping consoles and the low growl of powerful engines blending into a chaotic symphony. Jack wrestled two steaming mugs of coffee from a sputtering machine. Before him, a monstrous sonar screen pulsed with cryptic blips and blotches—silent signals only he and his perpetually wired assistant, Chip, could decipher.
To one side, a tiny TV spat out a news report—a breathless female reporter, her perfectly coiffed hair threatening to unravel in the storm, jabbering about Hurricane Sebastian's wrath on St. Augustine.

On the other, a smaller screen displayed the soul-soothing carnage of Manchester United demolishing Liverpool. A testament to Jack's stubborn devotion both to scientific truth and the comforting chaos of English football.
He pushed a mug toward Chip, whose eyes never left

the sonar. The reporter shrieked, barely audible over the storm's roar, "Seventy-nine-mile-an-hour winds pummeling St. Augustine! Waves hammering the beaches… storm surge flooding the streets… old St. Augustine fighting back, brick by brick, stone by stone…" Her manicured finger stabbed at a weather map tracking the hurricane's westward crawl. "But the worst, folks, should be over within the hour."

Jack reached for the remote to silence the well-meaning but irrelevant commentary, only for Chip to snatch it first.

"Hey! It's the crucial moment! Fergie time!"

Jack smirked, years melting away as the primal joy of football fandom eclipsed the weight of the mystery before them. He wrestled the remote back, plunging the reporter into blessed silence.

"I think you want to see this, Chip."

He pointed a calloused finger at the sonar, a knot tightening in his gut. "Got some serious weirdness here."

"Been running since we left port," Chip said, voice tight with calm barely masking manic energy.

"Keeps my left brain from melting down, you know?"

A thin, dark anomaly snaked across the screen—a deep, unnatural scar on the ocean floor.

Jack's breath hitched. "Depth's about two-fifty feet here, but this ravine… it drops off to eleven hundred. And it… shouldn't even be there."

"Shouldn't even be there," Chip echoed, gaze locked. They exchanged a look—a silent nod to the impossible.

Jack grabbed the satphone, fingers flying over the

speed dial. "Hey, guys, stand by for course change. Prepare for a hard stop!"

Bobbi, their ship's mate and co-pilot—a petite powerhouse from South Central LA, forever in impossibly short shorts and combat boots—grabbed a clipboard like a seasoned soldier.

Greg, equally sharp at the helm, responded instantly. "Ready, Cap."

"Two-nine-point-sixty-four North, eighty-point-sixty-six West," Jack barked, voice raw with urgency. "Bring us to a full stop."

"Copy that," Greg replied, eyes wide as he and Bobbi exchanged a quick, bewildered glance at the coordinates.

The ocean held its breath—and so did they.

Later, back at the marina, the video played on the iPad. Even through the screen, the galleon's image was breathtaking—massive, haunting, frozen in time.

"That," Greg breathed, voice thick with awe, "is one big ship."

Jack's eyes narrowed, voice low and reverent. "See the height of the stern? No doubt about it—a galleon."

"A Spanish galleon?" Chip murmured, a chill tracing down his spine. The implications were staggering, impossible to ignore.

"If we can get enough footage," Chip said, eyes glittering with greed, "this could make one hell of an episode. Your dad would love it!" He turned to Jack with a sly grin. "Hey, Jack — you know how to say

'galleon' in Spanish? A grand boatload of gold, eh?"
Jack shot him that look—that unmistakable 'you're
completely whacked' glare, forged through years of
shared danger and lunacy.
Greg grinned, undeterred. "A man can dream, can't
he?" But even as he said it, the dream felt too vivid,
too real, already pulling them deeper than they'd
bargained.
The possible weight of lost history fell on their
shoulders. In an instant, the reality of what lay
before them shocked them back into coherence.
 Jack and Chip's eyes snapped to the ravaged
shoreline—a grim tableau of splintered timber and
overturned boats clinging desperately to battered
docks.
The ORCA shuddered to a stop.
Sam's hands moved with surgeon-like urgency,
untangling tow lines. Bobbi, a blur of motion,
exploded off the bridge, her presence as vital as
oxygen in the chaos.

Then, the sight that stole their breath: a churning
expanse of lifeless fish—thousands, maybe millions,
a ghastly, silvery carpet smothering the water. Jack
and Chip stared, faces drawn tight with dawning
dread.
"THIS," Jack roared, voice raw and heavy with
looming disaster, "is not good."
"Unparalleled analysis required," Chip snapped.
"Grab water samples. Check oxygen levels. NOW!"
"On it!"
Jack's gaze swept the marina, his body rigid, a cold
tremor running through him. Chip followed his line

of sight, his blood turning to ice.

Two docks away, on the dark silhouette of the Sea Wench, a volatile scene exploded. Treese and Davis, locked in a brutal confrontation with a hulking man—menace carved in bone and muscle, his forties, eyes like coals—teetered on the edge of violence.

Jack turned away, a silent scream lodged deep in his throat. Chip caught the sign: *SEA WENCH MARINE SALVAGE*—an ironic label, chilling in its grimness. The man lunged, lips twisted in a snarl, finger stabbing into Treese's chest like a poisoned dart. Davis moved lightning-fast—a right hook cracking like thunder against the man's jaw. Surprise flashed in the brute's eyes, then blind fury.

Davis unleashed a brutal ballet of fists, hammering the man's head and ribs. The giant collapsed, a broken heap on the deck. Without hesitation, Davis rifled the man's pockets, producing a heavy plastic bag with nine gleaming gold coins. He tossed it to Treese with cold detachment.

"This should just about cover it," Davis said, flat and remorseless.

Treese's face remained unreadable. His eyes locked with Jack's across the distance, a venomous scowl twisting his lips—a silent, deadly threat hanging in the heavy air.

St.Augustine

Cold dread seized Chip. He scrambled after Jack, the thud of his heart pounding in rhythm with the fast, heavy footsteps behind him. Jack moved like a storm barely held in check, fury simmering beneath a brittle mask of calm. His shoulders were stone, jaw set tight as he marched toward the port-side ramp.
"Jack?" Chip hissed.
"His name's Romer Treese," Jack said, flat and cold. "Salvage? Please. I don't buy it for a second."
Chip froze. Intimidated by the scene across the marina. He could feel Terese's glare burn through him. Jack's tone was razor-sharp. "He's a mercenary. Dangerous. Met him once, a year ago. His brother... used to work with us."
Chip snapped his fingers, and the memory slammed into place. "Treese... Treese... oh, crap. That's *him*?" His gaze drifted to the dock, locking on something or someone. His breath caught. "Yeah," he whispered. "We're not sharing beers anytime soon."
Jack stopped dead at the top of the ramp. He grabbed Chip's arm, grip like a vice.
"Listen to me, Instagram. Tomorrow, we dive that wreck. If there's anything down there—and I'm betting there is—we identify the ship and file a claim in federal court. That's the law."
Jack's eyes burned into his.
"But this stays between us. Keep your mouth shut and that phone in your pocket. Got it?"
Chip just nodded, stunned.

Without another word, Jack turned and walked off. Chip slipped below deck, silence swallowing his footsteps.

Jack continued down the ramp, a storm churning behind his eyes. As he passed *Sea Wench*, Treese's glare tracked him—dark, sharp, and venomous.

Davis stood nearby, arms folded, a muscle twitching in his jaw as Jack disappeared down the dock. "Shouldn't that idiot be rotting in a cell?" Davis growled, his voice tight with barely contained rage. Romer didn't flinch. He stood motionless, the silence around him cold and deliberate.

"Genius is eternal patience," he said quietly, a dangerous glint in his eye. "But I suspect our wait will be short."

Jack moved quickly down the dock, like a man being chased by ghosts. His thoughts churned, sharp and chaotic. In the parking lot ahead, he froze. Standing near his Jeep was a figure that stopped him cold—Dr. Breanna Bonilla. Sun-kissed, sharp-eyed, and radiating danger beneath a Florida State cap and short shorts, she looked like she belonged on a magazine cover, not in the middle of his unraveling life. Her nervous energy pulsed in the air.

She was breathtaking—athletic grace, a long ponytail flicked by the wind, and those sharp, librarian glasses that always masked something deeper. Jack felt like the ground might give way beneath him. He forced himself forward, his pulse hammering in his chest.

"Hola, Jack," she said gently, her voice soft against
the storm still raging inside him.
He said nothing. Silence pressed between them,
heavier than anything he might have said.
"Will thought you could use some help," she offered,
her words tinged with hesitation.
His eyes met hers, raw and unreadable. "So, he sends
you?" he muttered. "You two on a first-name basis
now?"
He fumbled with his keys, the movement stiff and
unsteady, and pushed past her to unlock the Jeep.
"Breanna, please," he said, barely above a whisper,
his voice brittle with exhaustion. "Do us both a favor.
Go back to Miami."
She stood there, stunned, watching as he climbed in
and drove off, the engine's roar trailing behind him
like the end of a sentence neither of them wanted to
finish.

The old city gate of St. Augustine stood firm, defiant
against the battered landscape. Fallen trees
sprawled like defeated soldiers across the streets,
their limbs tangled in pools of murky water. San
Marcos Avenue was choked with debris—shattered
signs, broken glass, and fragments of lives upended.
Buildings bore their wounds openly, windows
boarded or blown out, walls scarred by wind and
water. Yet amid the wreckage, the city pulsed with a
raw, determined energy.
Work crews moved like an army of resilience, armed
with chainsaws, shovels, and sweat-soaked resolve.
They carved order from chaos, clearing a path

toward the Castillo de San Marcos, the ancient fortress watching silently over it all.

Sheriff Tom Heller stood like a weathered monument amid the destruction, a figure carved from grit and sun. His battle-scarred F-150 sat nearby, stacked incongruously with surfboards—symbols of calm defiance in the wake of the storm. One hand gripped a chainsaw, the other gestured with practiced command, directing the frenetic cleanup. A throwback in board shorts, sandals, and his rumpled uniform shirt, Tom looked every bit the Jimmy Buffett disciple, but his eyes, clear, steely, and unflinching, told a different story. He'd seen too much, and he wasn't blinking now.

"Just stack those logs on the curb!" he shouted, his drawl slicing through the humid air like a blade. The growl of tires interrupted the rhythm of chainsaws and shouted orders. Jack's Jeep rolled into view, headlights piercing the thickening twilight. It slid to a stop in front of Tom's truck like a challenge. Jack stepped out slowly, his figure framed in shadow before he emerged into the dusk.

Tom's face cracked into a grin—wild, unguarded relief.

"Alright...alright...alright," he said, hopping down from the truck. "Look who crawled outta the deep to save us landlubbers from drowning in pinewood." They embraced hard, no words needed. The hug said it all.

"Hey, Tommy," Jack said, his voice low and hoarse. He glanced around. "This... doesn't look so bad."

"Lucky," Tom rasped. "Power's out. Town's empty. But we dodged a bullet, Jack. Big one." He studied Jack's face. "When'd you get in?"

"Just now."

"I take it you went south. Found some kind of peace?"

"Sixty miles, give or take." Jack's gaze wandered to the horizon, where the ocean still writhed under the dying storm.

Tom followed his eyes, then moved to the back of his truck. He climbed onto the tailgate, casual but restless. Jack watched him, a silent question forming in the space between them.

Tom looked over his shoulder. "Nah. Nothing to do now. It'll be dark soon. But that surf?" He tapped the deck of his board with affection. "That surf's alive, Jack. It's calling. We've got time for one last ride before it calms."

There was something wild in his eyes—defiance, maybe, or reverence. A need to remind the storm who was still standing.

"Come on," he said, a grin tugging at the corner of his mouth. "You know you want to."

Jack hesitated, staring at the bruised horizon where water met sky. Then a slow smile crept across his face. It wasn't joy exactly—more like recognition. They weren't running from the storm. They were charging into its wake, one last time.

The sun hung low and molten, bleeding a bruised orange into a canvas of electric blue. The sky looked painted in heat and promise.

On the sand below, a volleyball game surged with barely restrained energy—a blur of tanned bodies in motion. Two men, lean and sharp-edged, moved with a coiled intensity, their eyes flashing with something more than competitiveness. Across the net, four women met them with easy laughter, their movements fluid and confident. But beneath the smiles and playful spikes, something simmered. It wasn't just a game—it was a quiet battle of dominance, a clash of wills masked by sunlit charm.

The ocean thundered like a living beast, each wave a monstrous wall of churning water, eight, maybe ten feet high, crashing down with bone-crushing force. Two lifeguards tore past on jet skis, neon blurs against the bruised horizon, their urgency a futile ballet against nature's fury.

Jack and Tom floated just beyond the break, straddling their boards like corks in the roiling sea. The salt spray slapped their faces. The air trembled with the weight of the waves, the roar pressing into their chests like a drumbeat.

"What's wrong, Bubba?" Tom called out, his voice barely slicing through the wind.

Jack exhaled, rough and low. "Breanna's back."

Tom winced. "Ouch." One word, laden with history.

"She said Dad thought I could use some help. Can you believe that?" Jack's laugh was joyless, his eyes fixed on the endless horizon.

Tom ran a hand through his wet hair, the gesture raw with frustration. "I always thought Dad needed me on the *Orca*. That's why I stayed. But lately... I

don't know. I don't think he trusts me anymore."
He let the silence stretch, then muttered, "Maybe I'll just start a band. I'm a better musician than a scientist anyway."
Tom grinned. "You play a mean guitar, alright. But you're more like the old man than you think."
"Oh yeah?" Jack muttered, shaking his head. His knuckles tightened around the edge of his board until they went white. For a moment, he seemed ready to snap—but then the fight drained from his shoulders, the defiance crumbling into something raw, something fragile.
"Your dad took his first expedition before his senior year," Tom said quietly, the memory laced with gravity.
Jack groaned. "God, no more stories."
"Just listen. He was gone for three months. Your mom broke off the engagement—over the phone, no less. And even then, that hard-headed handful wouldn't come home." Tom smirked faintly. "But a certain close friend gave them both a talking-to... and here you are."
Jack glanced sideways, his tone wary. "And?"
Tom placed a hand on his shoulder, the weight of it grounding. "You and your dad? Brilliant. No question. But when it comes to women..." He let the silence fill in the punchline. "You both couldn't find a light switch in the dark. And I mean that"
A flicker of a smile tugged at Jack's lips. A shared truth, simple and disarming.
"That so?" he said, but his gaze had already shifted, eyes narrowing on the approaching surge.

A monstrous wave loomed, a gleaming wall of fury building in the distance.

"Time to drop in," Jack said. It wasn't just a challenge—it was a surrender. A way to outrun the storm behind his eyes.

They paddled hard, in rhythm, bodies low and tense. The ocean's roar rose around them, relentless. Then the wave caught them, and everything else vanished. Their bottom turns were sharp, instinctive, slicing the face of the wave with practiced grace. They carved through the chaos, momentary masters of the violence beneath them.

And then the cycle again—paddle, drop, ride. Over and over. Each run is a fleeting heartbeat of clarity, of control, in a world that refused to be tamed. Another run. This one stretched longer, steadier—a shared triumph between Jack and Tom, the kind that didn't need words. Their rhythm, their timing, their instincts—it all clicked, a silent testament to experience and unspoken trust.

But then the sea shifted. A bigger wave surged from the depths, rising fast, too fast. It caught them off guard.

The wipeout was brutal. A violent tumble through the churning chop, limbs flailing, saltwater crashing into lungs and ears. It was a humbling jolt, a reminder that the ocean didn't care how skilled you were. It could take everything in a blink.

By the time they surfaced, coughing and winded, the sky was dimming. The horizon bled orange and violet, twilight settling in. A strange quiet fell between them, the kind born from exertion and awe. They floated in the lull, scanning the water, waiting. Each second stretched, nerves taut with anticipation.

Then Jack saw it.

The ten-footer.

It moved like a living thing, tall and smooth and fast, and his chest tightened—not with fear, but with that raw, primal thrill. For a moment, nothing else existed but that wall of water, that challenge, that pulse of life demanding to be met head-on.

"Kelly Slater can suck salt water! Watch this, Tommy!" Jack's boast was playful, but beneath the bravado lay a deeper truth—a fleeting moment of mastery, a hard-won triumph over the relentless ocean.

Tom's laughter rang out, full and free, a perfect echo of the shared joy between them. That camaraderie, forged in the wild heart of the sea, was something neither storm nor time could touch.

Together, they rode that final wave—a breathtaking dance of skill and timing, a perfect crescendo to a day carved from adrenaline and salt.

The ride back to shore was alive with energy: high fives, grins, the spark of connection ignited by shared risk and victory.

"Bubba, THAT was awesome! I almost forgot what a maniac you are." Tom's praise came wrapped in genuine awe, a nod to the wild edge Jack carried with him—the thrill of pushing limits, flirting with danger.

The casual mention of the "Surf-Master sheriff" was more than a joke; it was a quiet testament to a bond, a lineage of experience passed down through the endless roll of waves.

As they neared Tom's truck, the vibrant energy of the beach faded, replaced by the heavy weight of the day's aftermath settling over Jack. The exhilaration that had carried him moments before now slipped away, overtaken by unspoken anxieties and the looming reality waiting onshore.
The simple act of loading their boards onto the flatbed felt like a quiet ritual—a crossing from the boundless freedom of the ocean back into the confines of land, with all its unresolved tensions.
Tom's words hung in the air, more than mere advice: "Just talk to her, Jack — and remember, the Orca will always be your ship." It was a poignant reminder of inner strength, a call to find solace and resilience amidst life's storms.
Jack's uncertain expression betrayed the complex swirl of emotions inside him—the fading thrill of the waves wrestling with the daunting challenges waiting just beyond the horizon.

The Old Man And The Sea

In the heart of St. Augustine stood an old Spanish-style house, its air thick with the mingled scents of salt and aging wood—a fragrance both familiar and deeply poignant. Inside, a single room glowed warmly in the flickering candlelight.

Hector Sandoval, seventy-five years young and one of the city's revered figures, sat hunched before his easel. His dark, leathery skin told the story of a lifetime spent beneath the relentless sun. Around him, paints and brushes lay scattered in a colorful symphony.

On the canvas before him, four intricately detailed 16th-century Spanish galleons sailed with billowing sails, approaching a shadowed shore—a scene rendered with meticulous care and infused with a quiet, aching yearning.

A soft knock on the door broke the quiet spell. Hector moved slowly and deliberately, rising with a groan. His cane, a silent witness to the passing years, steadied him as he shuffled toward the door. His face creased into a gentle smile as he opened it. His English was careful and accented, a testament to years spent bridging cultures. "Gregory, I thought you were out to sea."

"Sí, but I'm back to check on mi Abuelo." Greg's attempt to mask his excitement was transparent. His embrace was warm, carrying a deeper, unspoken emotion.

"Todo bien?" Greg's question lingered, woven with

unspoken worries.

Hector closed the door with a weary shrug, a gesture heavy with the weight of years and quiet resilience. "Of course. It was just a little hurricane," he said, the lightness in his tone a fragile shield against deeper concerns.

Greg moved toward the easel, his gaze lingering over the dozen paintings—galleons battling tempestuous seas, the majestic Castillo de San Marcos, sun-drenched beach scenes—each brushstroke a whisper of memories, a life fully lived. His barely concealed excitement was palpable.

"Gregory," Hector's voice rumbled low, "you have good news, I can tell. Is it that girl... what's her name? Oh, sí, Dr. Bonilla. Are you two together again?" His question was laced with gentle curiosity, a grandfather's loving observation of his grandson's heart.

"No, no. We broke up before I moved back here to work on the Orca," Greg admitted hesitantly. "Pero, it was only a week or so." Regret, maybe even self-reproach, colored his words.

"Ah, but you liked her," Hector noted, his eyes twinkling with understanding. Time had not dulled his insight.

"Mira, Abuelo. Jack found a shipwreck—it looks like a galleon." Greg's voice brimmed with fresh hope. Hector's expression grew serious, history's weight settling deep on his face. "He's diving the wreck tomorrow." The simple statement carried the unspoken hopes and fears of dreams on the brink of reality.

Turning, Hector hobbled into the dining room—a room filled with years and memories, a museum of a lifetime. Greg followed, the air thick with dust, ghosts of forgotten stories hanging in the stillness. Past a table crowded with boxes, old canvases, and yellowed papers, rows of boxes stood three feet high along a far wall—a testament to a layered, lived life. Hector grabbed another flashlight, opened a closet door, and searched Greg's eyes.

"Por favor, don't get your hopes up," Hector warned, his voice a careful blend of wisdom and weariness. Beneath it lay a deep understanding of hope's fleeting nature and fate's unpredictable dance.

There was no immediate answer. Greg stepped into the cramped closet, reaching for a faded cardboard box.

A cascade of old papers tumbled down, whacking him square in the head.

He glanced at Hector, who just smiled—a smile heavy with the quiet wisdom of a lifetime, an unspoken acknowledgment of life's unpredictable twists, its joys and disappointments.

"Abuelo, two hundred seventy-five ships. Gone down around St. Augustine since 1535—just the ones we know about. The weight of that number... it settles over me. What are the odds, really? It feels almost... inevitable, like the sea itself claims what it's owed."

Greg hauled the box to the table, the wood creaking beneath the unseen burden. He set it down with a soft thud—a small counterpoint to the vast history the ocean held.

"If the odds are that high," Hector said, his voice trembling despite his effort to steady it, "why are you so excited?"

Silence filled the room, thick and expectant like mist drifting off the water. Greg found himself caught—not just in a lie, but in the swirling currents of his own fierce passion.

"Shipwrecks aren't just numbers, are they, Abuelo? They're echoes of lives lost, dreams shattered on unforgiving rocks. Each one a story whispered on the wind, a testament to human ambition and the sea's relentless power. It doesn't matter if they're French, English, or Spanish. Each find is a piece of a larger puzzle, a fragment of our shared history, reclaimed from the depths."

Greg ran his fingers through his hair, the weight of it all pressing down but fueling the fire inside.

"So, if this turns out to be *La Nuestra Señora de las Olas* or *Trinite,* you're good with that?" Greg asked, searching for a flicker of something unreadable in Hector's eyes.

"Oh, sí," Hector answered—too quickly, too smoothly. The casualness felt like a fragile mask, barely hiding something deeper. Greg laughed—a sharp, brittle sound—then opened the box with a defiant flourish, a challenge to the heavy weight of expectation and the ghosts lurking in the past.

"Liar," Greg teased, the word hanging between them like smoke, a reflection of his own doubts and the tangled complexities beneath the surface.

Hector reached in slowly, lifting out an old ship's bell.

Its tarnished surface caught the dim light, faintly gleaming like a relic from another world. The simple act of pulling it from the box felt monumental. He pushed the box aside and set the bell on the table. Greg's eyes caught the engraving—*Arabelle.* The name whispered from the depths, a ghost calling out through time. Both men paused, caught in the quiet mystery of the bell's story—of the lives it had witnessed, the fate it had survived.

A dark road stretched ahead, wind howling like a wild symphony as Jack gripped the wheel of his Jeep, fighting for control.

He swerved sharply, narrowly missing two colossal trees toppled by the storm's fury.

At last, the battered vehicle shuddered to a halt before a looming warehouse—*LAPOINTE OCEANIC RESEARCH*—its faded letters barely visible beneath the relentless downpour. Hurricane shutters clamped the windows like steel eyelids.

Jack snatched a flashlight, plunging the Jeep's cabin into darkness before stepping out into the night. The world around him dissolved into a black, drizzly void, pierced only by the frantic beam of his light as he raced toward the building. The lock clicked—a brittle sound swallowed by the roar of wind whipping through the low oak trees—and he slipped inside.

The office was a tomb. The only light, a sickly green glow from a rear exit sign. Jack moved with grim purpose, a shadow threading through the darkness straight to the lab door.

Inside, the silent laboratory swallowed his footsteps, each echo stark against the oppressive quiet, until he reached the generator panel. One flick of a switch, and the lab burst to life—a sudden eruption of light and the steady hum of awakening computers and monitors.

His eyes settled on the wall—a stark collision of scientific triumph and tender family memory. Will and Jack's doctorate diplomas in Marine Biology, proudly framed beside their Navy diving certificates—a shared ambition now fractured. A photograph froze a happier time: Will, young Jack at ten, little Billy at six, and their mother, a radiant blonde glowing with impossible serenity. Other pictures showed teenage Jack in scuba gear, camaraderie with Billy and Will aboard the Albatross's bridge.

He sank into the chair before the large flat screen. A glance at the smaller monitor, a few precise mouse clicks, and the big screen flickered on—revealing a desolate, inky abyss of ocean floor. Two beams of light sliced through the darkness, exposing grotesque methane bubbles seeping from fissures below. Depth: 6,354 feet. A terrifying depth. Then the screen died, melting into a chaotic blizzard of static.

Suddenly, a two-way video call snapped into view— a jarring contrast to the lab's oppressive silence. Will's face filled the screen, worry etched into every line. "Jack, is that you?"

Jack's grim face appeared in reply. "Yep. Came to

inspect the lab. We're running on generators, but everything else looks good."

Will's voice tightened, suspicion barely veiled. "How long have you been watching?"

A chilling pause stretched between them. Then Jack's voice broke the silence:

"Long enough to know you found another methane hydrate bed."

Will's reply was swift, icy.

"I'm logging off."

"Why?!" Jack's voice cracked, raw with anguish.

"Because you're not on board with the facts."

Jack's tone sharpened, defiant.

"I *know* what the facts are, Dad. Multiple studies shows that global warming and cooling are driven by fluctuations in the sun's heat."

Will ignored him, eyes flicking to a stack of papers.

"Sure, methane levels are rising, but I think you're overstating..." His voice trailed off, defeated. "You're not even listening, are you?"

Weariness weighed heavily on Will's face—deep lines carved by sorrow.

"It wasn't easy, raising you and your brother alone. But remember those summers on the Albatross? I miss those days. It was... fun."

Jack's eyes glazed, reflecting the pain of a thousand unspoken words. The memory of sun-drenched afternoons felt like a cruel mockery of his fractured present.

"Ever since Billy died," Will's voice dropped to a whisper, "it feels like you have to fight me on everything. I'm telling you one more time—I don't

blame you for what happened. Not for any of it."
The monitor went black. Silence engulfed the room, pierced only by Jack's ragged breathing. His face was a mask of torment, grief, and guilt pressing down on him, heavier than any storm.

Jack's thoughts drift back to that day that lives etched in his memory forever.
Breanna's knuckles whitened against the console as she stared into the flickering monitor. Behind her, Jack loomed like a shadow, his hands pressing into her tense shoulders with a brutal, almost frantic grip. He said nothing. The grainy, static-riddled image on the screen was a fragile window into the abyss. Inside the cramped submersible cockpit, Billy LaPointe's feverish excitement cut through the interference, while Malcolm Treese's grim face brooded beside him.
Billy's voice crackled through the comms, strained but alive.
"Three thousand feet, Jackie boy. It's… tight down here. Never been this deep before." "What's the visibility, Malcom?" Jack's voice
muffled through the static.
A nervous, cruel laugh escaped Treese's lips.
"Visibility? What you'd expect at the bottom of the world. Pitch black. Except for… things." His words lingered, heavy with unspoken dread, barnacles clinging to the hull of their nerves.
Breanna reached back, her touch fleeting, tracing Jack's hands. A cold diamond glinted on her finger— a glittering promise mocking the chill that spread through the room. Jack's grin was tight, a strained rictus. Sliding into the seat beside her, silence fell

between them, thick, heavy with unspoken tension.
"Any venting from the trench, Treese?" Jack's voice dropped to a growl, barely audible over the hiss of the comms.
"Negative. Let's push it. Go deeper." Treese's tone shifted, forceful, almost defiant.
Breanna's breath hitched. She glanced at Jack—her wide eyes pleading, hope blooming and then crumbling under the weight of everything left unsaid.
Jack slammed the mute button. "What?" he whispered, rough, and edged with panic, he tried to hide.
Breanna's voice, barely above a whisper, sliced through the tension.
"This is it, Jack. A subduction zone capable of unleashing an 8.0… a chance to understand it all." Her gaze locked on his—a silent plea hanging between them.
Jack clenched his jaw.
"How deep is the Puerto Rico Trench?" he asked, not waiting for her reply. "Twenty-eight thousand feet! One methane burst and they're gone. The submersible's a coffin at that depth!"

Breanna interrupted, steady, colder now.
"Twenty-six thousand." Her correction hung stark in the air, defiant and unwavering.
Their eyes locked—a silent battle waging beneath the surface. The silence stretched taut, unbearable. Then a chilling smile curved Breanna's lips.
"My doctorate's in Marine Biology, Jack. Just like yours."
Jack's frustration boiled over. Her touch,

maddeningly soothing, pressed against the raw edges of his terror.

"It's okay," she whispered, a silken lie.

"Billy and Malcolm know what they're doing."

Jack wrestled with his conscience, fear a tangible weight in the cramped room. He hit unmute, voice strained, turmoil breaking through.

"Malcolm, what do you wanna do?"

Malcolm's curt reply left the choice to Jack:

"It's your show."

Billy's excited shout cut through the tension.

"C'mon, bro! This is where earthquakes are born!"

Their faces glowed on the monitor—expectant, desperate—a silent plea directed at Jack.

Breanna's whisper was urgent, desperate.

"Jack... they can do this."

Seconds stretched into eternity as Jack's mind raced, calculating risk and reward. Then his gravelly, strained voice shattered the silence:

"Take her in... but no deeper than four thousand."

A brittle smile flickered on Breanna's lips. Billy erupted in manic cheers.

"Alright! Alright! Alright!" Malcolm gripped the controls, knuckles white.

"Bet your bro would love this," Billy shouted over the din.

"Romer?" Malcolm chuckled hollowly, a ghost of a smile.

"Oh yeah... he'd be stoked."

The submersible plunged, swallowed by the inky blackness of the narrow canyon. The image vanished into shadow.

Jack and Breanna stayed glued to the monitor, faces bathed in eerie light. Their eyes widened as the narrow trench yawned open, revealing a breathtaking vista—a chasm of unimaginable depth, a stunning, deadly maw.

"Check... it... out. Amazing." Malcolm's voice trembled, barely audible over the static.

"Depth is thirty-nine eighty...and falling," Billy reported.

"That's enough, guys. Time to come home." Jack's words hung heavy, thick with dread.

"Jack, no. They've got room to maneuver now." Jack caught Breanna's gaze—defiance flickering in his eyes, quickly masked by a chilling calm.

"What's with you?" Her voice sharpened, edged with anxiety.

"They've got this." Jack forced a brittle laugh, leaning back as the chair creaked under his apprehension. Breanna's sly, predatory smile pushed him closer to the edge.

"Okay, okay. Malcolm, DO NOT go past five thousand, understood?" His voice cracked, a desperate prayer whispered into the void.

Billy laughed—a harsh, hysterical sound swallowed by mounting tension.

"Roger that." The curt reply was chillingly void of The submersible shuddered violently, a sickening groan vibrating deep in Malcolm's bones.

Panic clawed at his throat—cold, relentless, suffocating. Outside the viewport, thick water churned with frantic methane bubbles, a swirling froth alive with ghastly, iridescent eyes that seemed to stare down their doom.

"Heavy methane venting! Depth five thousand six hundred! We're losing pressure!" Malcolm's voice was a strangled rasp, barely piercing the deafening howl of escaping gas.

"Pull up! Pull up! For God's sake, pull up!" Jack's voice, usually steady and calm, shattered into shards of desperation.

Breanna gasped silently, eyes wide, frozen by the raw terror that only imminent death can summon.

Billy's face twisted from stoic professionalism into a grimace of primal fear.

Malcolm wrestled with the controls, each frantic movement a prayer. The sub—a cold metal coffin hurtling toward oblivion—buckled and spun wildly like a bronco thrown by an unseen hand. The canyon wall loomed ahead, a monstrous jagged cliff swallowing them whole.

"C'mon, c'mon... please..." Malcolm's breath hitched, a desperate whisper lost amid the cacophony of crashing metal and rushing water.

Then—a guttural roar ripped through the cockpit. Shards of shattering glass and rending metal screamed through the air. A horrifying crack spiderwebbed across the viewport, spreading like a malignant curse over the fragile barrier between them and the crushing abyss. Another crack, and another, until the glass was a fractured mirror reflecting their impending death. Billy and Malcolm stared, frozen, eyes locked on the spidering fractures
 as their hearts hammered a frantic tattoo against their ribs.

The world exploded. The viewport imploded, showering the cockpit in a lethal rain of shards.

Ocean surged in—a torrential, icy deluge.

Chairs ripped from their moorings, flinging Malcolm and Billy like ragdolls. Their bodies slammed into

the back wall with bone-crushing force.
The monitors died, plunging everything into darkness. A scream tore through the silence—raw, piercing, heart-wrenching. Breanna's scream. "Billy!"

The blank monitor stared back at Jack like an accusing void, mocking his numb despair. Breanna's tears didn't just fall—they cascaded, a torrential downpour echoing the catastrophic collapse that had shattered their world. Each drop struck the silence like a hammer blow, a grim rhythm matching the frantic pounding of blood in Jack's ears. His fingers hovered over the keyboard, trembling like a condemned man awaiting the executioner's axe. The air around them crackled with unspoken blame, the silence thick and suffocating—an invisible pressure cooker on the verge of explosion.
Then, with agonizing slowness, Jack began to type. Each keystroke was a ragged breath, a desperate plea to hold back the creeping darkness.
Suddenly, the screen flickered to life. "CALLING ALBATROSS" blazed across the monitor—a cruel beacon of false hope against the abyss that threatened to swallow them whole. Will's face appeared, his smile a grotesque mask of normalcy, too bright, too forced, hiding the storm raging behind his eyes. But the smile shattered instantly when Jack's voice broke through, raw and strangled. Devastation hung heavy between them, a silent scream pressing down like a physical weight, suffocating the air itself. Will's smile cracked, spiderwebbing into a terrified grimace as his eyes widened in horrified disbelief. The perfect façade crumbled, replaced by pure, unfiltered terror.

"What's wrong?" Will gasped, the question tearing through the silence like a gunshot.

Jack fought for breath, each word a mortal struggle **63**against the overwhelming despair.

"Dad... Billy and Malcolm... they... they were caught in a methane release... at fifty-six hundred feet..."

His voice shattered, dissolving into a choked sob. Will's hands clenched into fists, the careful composure he'd built collapsing into dust.

"What?" The word hung in the air, laden with the unbearable weight of loss.

"They... they imploded." Jack's voice was a horrified whisper, a desperate search for meaning where none could be found.

Breanna sat frozen, a statue carved from raw fear and crushing guilt. Her wide eyes, empty and glassy, mirrored the horror that consumed her. Jack's silent plea for her to speak, to share the unbearable burden, went unanswered. She was trapped within her own mind, suffocated by the chilling knowledge of her role.

"I... I gave the order. It was my decision." The words hovered in the heavy silence like a death knell, echoing through the digital void between them.

Jack stared at his reflection—a ghost trapped in the cold glow of the monitor. His face, carved by a thousand sleepless nights, wore grief like a second skin. He shakes his head in the hope of erasing the memory of that day.

"Jack?" A soft voice sliced through the heavy silence, tentative and fragile.

A violent shudder rippled through him. He spun around, eyes wild, desperate. Breanna stood framed in the harsh fluorescent light of the doorway—an unwelcome specter haunting the room.

"Mind if I come in?" Her words hung like a whispered threat.

Jack couldn't believe it. He spun the chair away in a frantic gesture. Breanna crossed the room, the silence thickening between them, amplifying every unspoken accusation. She sat down. The silence that followed was suffocating—dense and nerve-wracking, as she chose her words with agonizing care.

"I said, no." Her voice was a low whisper, bitter regret dripping from every syllable. Silence swallowed the room, screaming louder than any words could.

Breanna waited—a predator toying with her prey. "Did you hear what I said? Your dad wanted me back last month—and I said no." Her voice dripped with self-justification, a flimsy shield against the storm brewing behind her eyes.

"And yet you're still sitting here." Jack's voice dropped dangerously low, rage simmering beneath a controlled surface.

Breanna's face tightened, guilt flickering like a weak flame, failing to mask the cold calculation lurking beneath.

"You know, I was ready to take the hit. I'm the Captain. It was my responsibility. But you… of all people… should've had my back. I was covering for you!" The words hit like poisoned darts, venom in every syllable.

"Jack, I—" Breanna faltered, nerves unraveling.

"What, Breanna? What?" His voice cracked, the dam threatening to break. "I know I should've stayed, but—" She tried to explain, but her words were swallowed by—

Jack slammed his fist against the console—a violent, desperate blow that shattered the fragile calm.

"Billy and Malcolm are dead! My father barely talks to me! Romer Treese would kill me if he could! And the person I loved most… walked away! You walked away! That's what I live with every day!" His words exploded, a raw, unfiltered torrent of pain and fury. He stood, shaking, unable to hold himself together any longer. Turning his back to her, to the ghosts that haunted him. "And why," he spat each word like a venomous strike, "why didn't you ever tell my dad what really happened?"

The silence that followed was thick, suffocating. Breanna's ragged breath was the only sound. Her eyes, heavy with guilt, flicked away, searching for any escape from the storm raging between them.

"So now I'm supposed to forget all that? Trust you again? After… after everything?" His voice cracked, raw and strained.

"I hated myself, Jack," she whispered, barely audible over the pounding of his heart. "I still do. And every day, I watched what it did to you—what I did to you…" Her words faded, weighed down by all the things left unsaid.

"Then why the hell did you come back?!" His roar hit her like a blow, disgust twisting his features.

He shook his head slowly, a low growl rumbling deep in his chest.

To himself, he thought, Great move, Dad.

Reaching into his pocket, he moved deliberately, agonizingly slow. Then, with a heavy clang, he dropped a set of keys onto her lap.

"We sail at 0700 tomorrow," he said, his words clipped and sharp, like shards of broken glass. "With or without you."

Without another word, he stormed out the door slamming behind him like a guillotine.

Breanna sank into the chair, the weight of the keys burning through her clothes. Her reflection in the dark monitor stared back at her —

The words clawed relentlessly at Breanna's mind, pounding like a deafening drumbeat of self-loathing. The weight of their shared tragedy wasn't just pressing down on her—it was crushing her, suffocating her, leaving her gasping for breath in a world stripped of hope. The cold, metallic keys resting in her lap had become an instrument of torment, chilling reminders of an irrevocable act life sentence to a personal hell she could neither escape nor forget.

Flotsam And Jetsam

Outside, torrential rain flooded the parking lot in sheets. A splash of water erupted as a pickup truck tore through the standing puddles, its Harley-Davidson strapped to the rear bed, chrome gleaming faintly beneath the downpour. The truck slid to a stop behind another pickup already parked in front of the open Dive and Tackle store. The heavy scent of salt and wet canvas clung to the air, thick and unmistakable.

Romer Treese shifted his truck into park, eyes catching sight of Sam. Not just tossing two dive tanks into his truck bed, but arranging them meticulously among eight others nestled neatly inside—each one gleaming, almost new. Sam slammed the rear bed door shut with a sharp clang that cut through the rain's steady roar. He climbed into his truck and pulled away, leaving a spray of muddy water behind him.

Treese's boots were soaked through as he jumped out and sprinted toward the store, his movements quick and purposeful despite the storm. The window sign, blurred by rain-streaked glass, read: *WE BUY GOLD.* Beneath it, a smaller, almost illegible note added: *Discreet transactions a specialty.*

Lights blazed inside, revealing a surprisingly spacious interior. The low hum of a generator vibrated through the floorboards, filling the air with a steady thrum. A faint scent of ozone mingled with the mustiness of old wood. Treese stepped forward, his eyes scanning the display case packed with fishing lures—some tarnished and aged, others pristine and gleaming. Behind the counter, shelves groaned under the weight of diving gear and nautical charts.

From a back room that looked more like a workshop, an older man emerged. Hank, weathered and tanned from years under sun and salt spray, held a small, intricately carved wooden box in his hands. His lined face was creased by decades of hard living, his voice a low rumble as he greeted Treese.

"What's it gonna be today, Romer?"

Treese produced a plastic bag, its contents glittering in the dim light—five gold coins, their weight solid and real as he laid them carefully on the counter. Hank's eyes lit up with a sly grin, amusement flickering in his gaze. He pulled out a tarnished brass magnifying glass and inspected the coins with practiced precision, holding them up to the rain-filtered light streaming through the window. When he lowered the glass, a flicker of respect softened his expression.

"Mint 1857 Gold Eagles. I'm not even gonna ask," he murmured, tracing a finger along the intricate designs.

"Good life choice. So, you want them all? Say twenty-eight hundred each?"

Hank's tone was businesslike, but the smile never left his lips—almost eager to seal the deal.

"You got yourself a deal," Treese replied.

With that, Hank slid open a surprisingly deep, well-organized drawer and began counting stacks of neatly wrapped hundred-dollar bills. The sharp scent of fresh ink blended with the salty sea air. Treese's gaze drifted to a half-hidden map pinned on the wall, marked with a jagged coastline and dotted with X's and cryptic symbols.

"The kid who just left here," Treese asked quietly, "isn't he from the Orca? The one that disappeared six months ago?"

Hank finished counting, expression flat and unreadable now. Before handing over the stacks, he made a subtle scratch on one of the bills—an invisible mark of some secret code.

"Everybody wants to be a treasure hunter," Hank said, a quiet warning woven through his words. Treese smirked, clearly taking the message. He gathered the cash and slipped Hank a gleaming silver dollar, its surface nearly flawless. Hank's practiced detachment shattered in an instant; he almost dropped the coin, eyes wide with genuine surprise.

As Treese stepped out into the rain, Hank muttered with newfound respect, "You're a good man, Romer." Climbing into his truck, Treese shut the door and slid the key into the ignition. Then his face darkened, the mood shifting like a storm cloud. He pulled out his battered phone and swiped to a photo—a snapshot of himself and a man named Malcolm, laughing amidst a haze of cigar smoke and empty beer bottles. The image felt too cheerful, too staged.

Slowly, outrage seeped into Treese's expression as his fists were clenched tight on the steering wheel.

From the far end of the parking lot, Treese's truck roared to life, tires splashing through puddles and sending muddy spray into the air. Tom watched from his own truck—the Sea Wench Marine Salvage 's name boldly painted across the side—as he turned the ignition key with a wary glance. His face was tight, grim, the weight of unspoken thoughts pressing behind his eyes. Without hesitation, he followed, the rain pouring steadily around them, washing away footprints and traces but leaving the questions stubbornly unanswered.

The humid air hung heavy over St. Augustine Municipal Marina, clinging to the salt spray with a cloying sweetness even after the rain had passed. A brutal offshore wind, sharp with the scent of brine and something vaguely metallic, whipped across Sam's face as he struggled to wrestle the last two dive tanks onto the Orca's pitching deck. Chip sidled past, his eyes fixed everywhere except on the hard manual labor.
"Seriously, Chip? You could've helped." Sam's voice was a low growl, his hands raw from gripping the corroded metal. Ten tanks now sat piled on the deck, a metallic mountain at Chip's feet. Chip winced, eyes widening suddenly as something beyond Sam caught his attention. "Uh-oh."
Sam spun around. Treese. Just the name tasted like bile on his tongue. The man swaggered up the ramp,

a wicked glint in his eyes, the polished gleam of a hunting knife stark against the cheap denim clinging to his lean frame. The scent of stale sweat and cheap cologne — and something darker, something feral — clung to him like a shroud.

"I'd rethink any underwater activities if I were you boys," Treese sneered, his voice a venomous rasp. "Your captain's safety record ain't exactly stellar. Hey, LaPointe! Sending these greenhorns to their watery graves, or finally grown a pair?"

The silence that followed crackled with menace. Then, like a coiled spring released, Jack LaPointe burst from the hatch below — a whirlwind of fury, his face a mask of white-hot rage.

"Get off my ship, Treese!" he roared, voice raw with barely contained violence.

Treese laughed, a chilling sound like nails on a chalkboard. "How's that still your ship, Jack? Oh right — good old Dad bailed you out. Again." He stepped closer, eyes icy. "Wanna roll, Treese? We can settle this right here, right now."

A vein throbbed in Jack's temple. "Whoa, that's a lot of rage, pal. And I don't appreciate threats from a guy with blood permanently staining his conscience."

Without warning, Treese ripped the knife free. The steel flashed under the stormy sky. He didn't just hold it — he hurled it. The blade whistled through the air, a sickening smack as it embedded itself inches from Jack's foot.

Sam lunged forward — then froze.

Jack's hand moved impossibly fast. A Glock

appeared, the cold steel glinting sharply. The metallic tang of gun oil filled the air, sharp and acrid.

"Last chance. Get off my ship." Jack's voice was flat, emotionless, colder than the ocean depths.

Treese stood his ground, daring him, the wind whipping his already crimson face.

Then a voice cut through the tension.

"Romer, I think you're confused."

Tom. The newcomer's presence was like a sudden shift in the weather — calm, yet carrying an authority even Treese couldn't ignore.

"Wrong ship, son."

Treese's glare at Jack was pure venom, a fleeting, predatory smile twisting the corners of his lips before he turned and stalked away. Jack's face remained a mask of barely controlled fury as he spun toward Sam and Chip, his voice low and guttural, issuing a sharp command.

"Get this gear below. Now."

Pale-faced and silent, Chip and Sam scrambled for the tanks, their movements frantic, as if each second counted for survival.

Tom clapped Jack on the shoulder with a grin. "Good thing I happened by. Think I just saved you from a whole lot of trouble. Pun intended."

Jack bent down and snatched the knife off the deck. The cold steel bit into his palm, burning with a familiar sharpness. He turned his gaze out to the turbulent sea, where the Sea Wench rocked restlessly against the dark waves. A cold certainty settled in his bones—this was only the eye of the storm.

Deep Dive

The Orca cruised out of port, its wake carving a churning ribbon across an unusually calm sea. Jack stood by the bow railing, hands jammed deep in his sweatshirt pockets, a frown carving itself deeper into his weathered face. The heavy air between them was thick with unspoken tension—a subtle dissonance that clashed with the steady thrum of the engines. Footsteps approached quietly on the steel deck. Chip's voice broke the silence, low and hesitant.

"Those fish died from oxygen depletion, right?"

Jack's gaze remained fixed on the distant horizon. "Like a heart attack. Elevated methane concentrations. But..." He hesitated, a flicker of doubt darkening his eyes. "The levels were... inconsistent. Too localized."

"Did you check the dive gear?"

"Sam handled it. Everything checks out... officially," Chip said, his tone clipped.

Breanna appeared then, her presence sudden and jarring, like a sharp note disrupting a symphony. She was back—not just physically, but with a new authority burning in her eyes. A small satchel hung from her shoulder, its contents unseen but heavily implied.

"What's with the dive tanks, Jack?" Her voice was sharp, slicing through the strained quiet. She strode toward them, unwavering.

Chip grimaced, muttering under his breath, "Ugh,

and why exactly is she back? This is a disaster waiting to happen.”

“Dad sent her,” Jack replied quietly, eyes flicking to the satchel.

“After the way she left? Not a fan, Boss. Not a fan,” Chip muttered, his unease clear.

Breanna’s voice cut in, tension rising. “What’s going on? This isn’t the methane hydrate survey.”

“Didn’t Chip tell you?” Jack’s voice held a trace of amusement.

“He said… he’s a steel trap,” Breanna narrowed her eyes, the phrase heavy with unspoken meaning.

Jack smirked, but the amusement faded quickly, replaced by a cold edge. “Finally sunk in. And why are we heading south? We’re supposed to be looking for methane hydrate beds north of the Outer Ridge. The coordinates… they were altered.” His voice dropped almost to a whisper, eyes wide with sudden, chilling understanding. Without another word, he pivoted and strode toward the hatch leading below deck, his movements brisk and determined.

“Jack!” Breanna called after him, but her voice was swallowed by the roar of the engines and the gathering storm of unease.

“Chip, have Sam bring the gear on deck. Then meet me in the lab,” Jack ordered, his voice calm but firm. Without waiting for a reply, he disappeared down the hatch. Breanna stood frozen, staring after him in disbelief. Her face was a mixture of confusion and dawning apprehension. The satchel slung over her shoulder suddenly felt heavier than it should. The once-calm sea outside now seemed threatening, the distant horizon a murky canvas filled with unanswered questions.

Inside the Orca's bridge, Bobbi monitored the sonar, its rhythmic pulses a steady counterpoint to the hum of the engines. Greg, at the helm, made subtle course adjustments, eyes scanning the darkened horizon. A faint, almost imperceptible anomaly flickered on the sonar screen — a blip that shouldn't be there, too deep and too consistent to be natural. Bobbi's gaze sharpened with concern as she pointed it out.

"Yo, Bobbi, take the wheel," Greg said, his voice sharper than usual.
Bobbi's hands tightened on the controls as she took over. Greg hurried off the bridge just as Breanna burst toward the hatch, her figure silhouetted against the moonlit waves. Bump. The impact was slight, but the shared shock was palpable.
"Greg?" Breanna's voice was breathless, laced with disbelief.
Greg forced a strained smile, pulling her into a brief hug. "Bree. What are you doing here?"
Breanna looked like she'd seen a ghost, her wide eyes darting nervously as if expecting someone to accuse her. "I was gonna ask you the same thing."
"I'm Orca's pilot. Been here four months." He paused, searching her eyes. "You working with Jack?"
She nodded silently, hesitation clear in her affirmation. Greg's hand caressed her shoulder

gently. "Muy bien. Muy bien. I'm glad you're here."
But the relief was short-lived. Breanna suddenly
recoiled, her eyes locked on something behind him.
"Don't be…" she whispered, her voice trailing off.
Greg spun around, eyes widening. Chip stood at the
edge of the deck, his usual jovial expression replaced
by stunned disbelief. His gaze locked intently on
Breanna. They exchanged a look — a silent, chilling
conversation heavy with unspoken understanding.
An unsettling current crackled between them.
Greg quickly retreated back onto the bridge,
slamming the hatch behind him. Chip's incredulity
was obvious, palpable even to the usually oblivious
"geek boy." The anomaly on the sonar screen
intensified, pulsing with a new, sinister rhythm.
"Well," Chip muttered low, "this is just a big bowl of
suck."

Breanna stepped into the control room, her usual
composure cracked by a nervous tremor in her
hands. Jack sat at the control panel, his face
unreadable.
"Here. See for yourself," he said, tapping the mouse.
The monitor sprang to life, displaying a complex
array of side-scan sonar readings. Breanna lingered
behind him, skepticism etched across her features.
Chip entered, carrying a portable mini-projector. As
he connected it and placed it on the console, Jack
glanced at him, a flicker of apprehension in his eyes.
"Hello?" Jack said.
"Sorry, what?" Breanna murmured, still fixated on
the intricate lines spreading across the screen.

"The sonar," Jack said quietly, his voice low and steady. "It's a galleon."

Breanna finally turned, eyes widening as she studied the sonar image. "Maybe."

"Maybe?" Chip cut in, a mischievous glint lighting his eyes. "Allow me to blow your mind."

With a tap, the projector sprang to life, casting a breathtaking 3-D color image of the galleon into the air. The detail was astounding — a vibrant reconstruction of a ship seemingly plucked straight from the ocean floor. Breanna gasped, circling the rotating image. The green outline of the galleon's hull was clear, its bow partially buried in sand, stark against the brown seabed and teal water. Purples and yellows highlighted the main deck and three lower decks, while a striking blue hole gaped near the toppled main mast. Dark greens accented the bridge. Twenty feet behind the ship, the seabed plunged into sudden blackness, a sharp contrast to the surrounding sediment.

"I've... I've heard whispers about this," Breanna stammered, struggling to grasp what she was seeing. "But to actually see it..."

"No," she shook her head, disbelief tightening her voice. "There's no way. A galleon would be three to four hundred years old. This wreck... it's in remarkably good condition. And that ravine... it's not even on any chart."

"Earthquake," Chip said simply.

Breanna stared at him, speechless. "Did everyone's IQ plummet while I was gone?"

"Hey, not cool," Chip retorted defensively.

"The ravine's there, isn't it? Got any brilliant ideas, genius?"

Breanna's indignant reply caught in her throat as Jack tapped the control panel. A video flickered onto the main monitor — the rover's point of view. A violent downdraft, strong enough to nearly pull Jack and Sam into the chasm, whipped across the screen. The rover spun wildly, capturing a fleeting glimpse of a shadow — a ship — revealed as sand swept away from a ridge. Swish! The rover hurtled past Jack and Sam, narrowly escaping the abyss.

"Before yesterday, she was buried — who knows for how long," Jack explained grimly. "Combine that with a methane hydrate bed that could have drastically slowed bacterial decomposition... it's as if she was preserved by some sort of underwater perfect storm."

Breanna stared at the screen, her face pale. "Jack, you could have been killed."

"Nah," Jack shrugged. "The hurricane just stirred things up. But Chip might be right. What else could have cleaved the seafloor like that?"

"An earthquake? Here?" Breanna whispered.

"It's the Bermuda Triangle," Chip grinned, manic energy flickering in his eyes. "The capital of bizarro world."

Breanna looked at Jack, his determined gaze fixed on the 3-D galleon. "So," he asked, challenge thick in his voice, "what do we do?"

The question hung heavy in the air: what secrets did this perfectly preserved galleon — and this newly revealed chasm — hold.

The Albatross

Somewhere in the open ocean, the distant whir of an approaching helicopter sliced through the vast silence, almost swallowed by the endless expanse. The research vessel *Albatross* rocked gently, anchored in deep waters, dwarfed by the immensity of the sea. Andros Island was a faint smudge on the horizon. The chopper's rotors grew louder, their relentless beat thudding like a drum against the quiet.

Curiosity flickered across their faces as Will and his tech specialist, a young woman named Anya, stepped onto the deck. They tracked the incoming black HH-3F Pelican amphibious helicopter, its sharp silhouette etched against the bright azure sky. Anya, already at her console, relayed data — the chopper's transponder was erratic, its flight path... unconventional. Will barked a terse order, and Anya's fingers flew across the keyboard, initiating a discreet counter-surveillance sweep.

The helicopter roared as it descended, settling heavily on the *Albatross*' stern. Its side door hissed open, revealing Raymond — a man whose expensive suit couldn't mask the tremor in his hand. He was the epitome of oil-slicked power, but his eyes betrayed something else — fear? Or something more calculating?

A small motorboat deployed from the chopper zipped toward the *Albatross*. Anya expertly lowered a rope ladder as the boat's wake disturbed the calm surface. Will, his face a mask of controlled fury, slipped below deck. As Raymond entered his quarters, the air thickened with unspoken tension. Their handshake was brief, cold, and impersonal.

"Bonjour, Will," Raymond began, his French accent heavy with practiced formality. "I assume you're not here for a... leisurely cruise?"

Will opened his mouth to respond, but Raymond cut him off, voice low and urgent. "You know damn well why I'm here."

"The board of directors didn't buy into my proposal?" Will asked, dangerously calm.

Raymond's gaze darted nervously around the room, as if hidden microphones lurked in every corner. "An understatement," he hissed. "The oil industry spends millions convincing the world that climate change is a non-issue. Did you really think we'd fund your... Extinction Protocol?" He paused, a chilling smile flickering on his lips. "I presented your idea. And now, I'd like to keep my job."

"But the data is irrefutable!" Will insisted, voice rising. "Rising methane levels are accelerating global warming. Deep-sea drilling makes it worse—"

"You're wasting your breath!" Raymond snapped, his fist clenching tightly. "We've been partners for twenty years. But this... this is different. Let it go, Will. Please."

"This is about public awareness!" Will shot back. "A chance to change the world! Who better than one of the biggest oil companies to lead the charge?"

Raymond's face twisted into a mask of controlled desperation. "This isn't about saving the planet, Will.

It's about survival — Big Oil's survival. The world is changing, and we're fighting to stay afloat. The board is terrified — terrified the public will believe you. Our investments… they're too important. We're out. I'm sorry."
Will's eyes narrowed. This wasn't just about Big Oil anymore. This was something far deeper.

The narrow cobblestone street lay cloaked in shadows, where ancient oaks stretched their gnarled branches overhead like silent sentinels. Somewhere deep in St. Augustine's tangled maze of streets, an old black pickup rested in a cracked driveway, its paint faded and chipped like a half-forgotten memory. The hood was thrown open, revealing a mess of rusted metal and tangled wires. Davis's face was smeared with grease as he leaned into the engine, gripping a wrench in his roughened hand. The heavy air smelled of salt and slow decay, hanging thick and oppressive.
Breaking the stillness, a guttural roar ripped through the quiet, shaking the cracked foundations of the old houses. The unmistakable thunder of a Harley roared closer, a fierce and primal announcement of arrival.
Treese pulled up behind the truck, his silhouette stark against the fading light. As he swung off his bike, a worn leather saddlebag swung open, revealing more than just *The Confidence Man* by Herman Melville. Nestled among the pages was a tarnished silver locket, its intricate carvings hinting at a forgotten language, a lost history.

"That hunk of junk didn't start before the storm hit. It's not gonna start now," Treese muttered, stepping away from his bike.

"Have a little faith," Davis replied, his voice a low rumble.

Treese produced a roll of hundred-dollar bills and slid it across to Davis. "This might help."

Davis counted the bills, a small grin tugging at the corner of his mouth. "Why don't you buy yourself one of these?" Treese asked, nodding toward the matte black beauty parked behind him.

"No flipping way," Davis laughed, the sound carrying something more than amusement. "You're fearless in the jungles of Honduras, facing down cartel bosses, but two wheels scare you?"

Treese smiled.

Davis smirked, a little chastened, and stuffed the money into his pocket. A strange apprehension settled over him.

"So, where's the next mission? Brazil? Mexico? Something involving ancient artifacts and hidden temples, perhaps?" Davis joked, trying to lighten the mood.

Treese was silent for a long moment, the setting sun casting long, dramatic shadows around them. He pulled out a portable GPS tracker. Instead of a simple address, the screen displayed a cryptic sequence of symbols and coordinates. He handed it to Davis.

"Something more local," he said. The message was clear.

The Mystery Beneath

The hot sun beat down relentlessly on the deck, a sharp contrast to the icy depths waiting below. No wetsuits were needed today; the air itself seemed to shimmer with heat. Breanna stood beside Jack, breathtaking in a steel-blue bikini that caught and reflected the sunlight like liquid metal. Around them, a tense, watchful circle formed. Chip and Bobbi moved with practiced efficiency—almost ritualistic—as they fastened black belts humming softly with the power of their battery packs around their waists.

"So that's the plan," Jack said low, his voice heavy in the thick air. "We're just going to scope her out." Sam's sharp, indignant gaze lingered on Breanna, but Greg was utterly captivated, his eyes fixed on her as she and Jack hefted their dive tanks. Breanna felt his stare—a confused, almost desperate intensity—but the knot of apprehension in her stomach held her from meeting his eyes.

Greg picked up a waterproof iPad, the sonar image of the galleon glowing with an eerie, ethereal light, its secrets locked away deep beneath the waves.

"Chip," Jack's voice cut through the simmering tension, "any sign of methane seeps, and we're outta there."

Jack pulled Sam aside with a quiet urgency. Chip followed, snapping sleek modular propeller thrusters onto Jack's forearms, their metallic surfaces gleaming as they clicked into place on the battery pack. They looked like something ripped from a futuristic war film—extensions of Jack's own body, recalling the armor of a certain iron-clad hero. Sam watched, awe and trepidation mingling on his face.

"Look," Jack murmured, "I know you wanted the dive, but she *is* the most qualified diver on this ship."

"It's fine," Sam muttered, eyes dropping to the strange devices strapped to Jack's arms. "What the heck are those?"

"The future, Sammy," Jack replied, a faint smile tugging at his lips. "The Navy's had them about a year now. They can push you up to eight miles per hour."

Sam's eyes widened. "I want one."

Bobbi's hands moved with precise, surgical care as she secured identical thrusters onto Breanna's forearms.

"Breanna, honey," Bobbi's voice softened, laced with a motherly concern that felt out of place amid the tension, "you be careful down there. Is this right?"

Breanna barely whispered, "Yeah, that's it."

Bobbi gave her a once-over, a knowing smile curling at the corners of her mouth.

"Ay, Mami," she murmured, leaning in close with a conspiratorial whisper. "You're slammin' in that tiny blue thing. The Cap's been missin' you, girl. It's good you came back."

Breanna visibly flinched, tugging at her bikini top, a ripple of discomfort passing over her face.

Jack watched the exchange, his expression hardening. The lighthearted mood from moments before seemed to evaporate, replaced by a tangible tension—the weight of the ocean's mysteries pressing down on them all.

Jack thought back to the dreadful day a year earlier. The rain fell steadily, slicking the blacktop with a cold, somber sheen. Jack moved forward, shoulders heavy with grief, each step weighed down by the crushing loss. The gleaming obsidian limousine awaited, its polished surface reflecting the gray sky. A cold hand suddenly touched his arm. He turned to see Breanna—her face carved with sorrow, eyes shimmering with unshed tears.
Slowly, deliberately, she slipped off her engagement ring. The diamond caught the faint sunlight, flashing cruelly—a mocking reminder of the happiness they once shared, now shattered. The ring rested in her palm like a tiny island of light amid a vast sea of despair.
Jack's gaze locked on the delicate gem. A strangled sob escaped him before he turned and walked away, the weight of the ocean's mysteries pressing down on them all. A sinking thought fell over Jack as his mind drifted back to his brother's funeral. Something else died that day.

The memory clawed at Jack, leaving him breathless and raw. Chip's voice shattered the haze of his anguish, sharp and unyielding.
"You're on a straight trimix blend, max depth 280 feet—and no speeding. Understand?" The words hung heavy in the thick, humid air.

Jack and Breanna stepped onto the dive platform. The metallic chill seeped into their bones, mirroring the icy grip of the unspoken resentments between them. The bulky SAT helmets were fitted snugly, hiding their faces but amplifying the tension simmering beneath the surface. Greg handed Breanna the iPad; its glowing screen was a stark contrast to the grim determination in her eyes. They exchanged a brief, agonizing glance—a silent acknowledgment of shared risk, lingering pain, and the unspoken questions hanging between them like a shroud. Breanna turned her head, her voice amplified and slightly distorted through the comm system, reaching across the chasm of their fractured relationship.

"Jack, you copy?"

Jack stared back, his face a mask of suppressed rage and gnawing heartache. A single word, heavy with emotion, escaped his lips.

"Yeah."

With a powerful push, he plunged into the cobalt depths, a silent rebellion against the sorrow threatening to consume him. Breanna followed, mirroring his despair. Their descent was a desperate attempt to escape the crushing weight of their past—a harrowing dive into the unknown depths of their future.

Below, Sam expertly lowered the Rover into the water. Chip's face was grim as he grabbed the remote and headset. The propellers churned, a mechanical heartbeat against the ominous silence, before the Rover vanished beneath the waves, leaving only ripples and unanswered questions in its wake.

Jack and Breanna sliced through the turquoise water, sleek and graceful. Around them, vibrant tropical fish swirled in a living, breathing rainbow. But the tension between them hung heavier than the humid air.

"After today," Jack whispered against the ocean's symphony, "I think you should go."

Breanna's reply was a heartbreaking echo of duty. "Can't do it, Jack. You know I only take orders from Will."

"When you're on my ship…" Jack began, voice tight with simmering frustration, but the comm system cut him off.

"I hear you both loud and clear," Chip's voice crackled, jarring them from their charged silence.

Jack and Breanna exchanged a look—a silent scream of mutual exasperation.

Breanna broke the tension with a burst of defiance. She spun underwater, executing a breathtaking series of pirouettes—four perfect 360s—ending with a gravity-defying triple circle through a shimmering school of bioluminescent fish. Jack watched, lips pressed tight, fighting back a grin that threatened to betray the gravity of their mission.

"Ease up, Tinkerbell," Jack said, voice laced with wry concern. "Thermocline dead ahead. Visibility's gonna be near zero."

They plunged into murkier depths, the current tugging with insistent power. Breanna tapped her iPad; sonar readings, depth, and temperature lit up the screen like a vital lifeline.

"We're good," she announced, steady despite the churning water and the unease creeping in.

They broke through the thermocline into clearer waters, only to find themselves dwarfed by the ominous shadows of two pairs of tiger shark eyes gliding silently just yards above. Jack's sharp tap on Breanna's arm, followed by a pointed finger, sent a jolt of icy fear racing through her. Her heart hammered wildly against her ribs—a frantic drumbeat echoing the rising tension around them.

Their speed eased as the Rover drew nearer, its dive lights casting long beams that illuminated a shape resting on the seabed—an apparition so vast it stole their breath away.

"There she is," Jack breathed, awe threading his voice.

"My God," Breanna whispered, overwhelmed by the sheer scale of what lay before them, the weight of history pressing down in the deep.

The majestic Galleon rose from the ocean floor, its bow half-buried in sand, the port side leaning against a rocky ridge, and its stern perched a mere twenty feet from the edge of a yawning ravine. It was a breathtaking sight, a silent monument to a forgotten era—and a prize fraught with danger. Jack's voice dropped to a low rumble, tight with anticipation. "You getting this, Chip?"

On deck, Chip sat cross-legged amid a tangled mess of cables and equipment, his eyes locked on the

glowing screen of his iPad. He didn't miss a single detail. Greg, Sam, and Bobbi gathered closely around him, their faces bathed in the soft blue light.
"Oh yeah," Chip said, his voice alive with excitement. "In full 4K."

Jack and Breanna moved closer to the gargantuan galleon, a colossal relic rising from the ocean's cold embrace. Breanna held her iPad steady, capturing the scene — a ghostly resurrection of a long-forgotten past. "History resurrected," Jack whispered, awe thick in his voice, the words catching in his throat.
They glided toward the bow, where a towering rigging pole jutted upward like a skeletal finger, barnacle-encrusted and weathered, a mute witness to the relentless march of time.
"Let's check out the port side," Jack murmured, his voice barely disturbing the ocean's quiet.

Treading water, Jack admired the majestic bow for a moment before propelling himself after Breanna and the Rover. As Breanna reached midship, a sudden, guttural gasp escaped her lips. A massive manta ray — dark and graceful — burst from a yawning hole in the hull, passing mere inches from her before disappearing back into the shadows below.
Jack surfaced silently behind her, his hand resting gently on her shoulder. Breanna shuddered, muttering a stream of Spanish curses under her breath. Jack let out a dry, ironic chuckle that mirrored the tension tightening the air around them.

"Boss, tic toc, tic toc," Chip's voice crackled through the comms, a reminder of the ticking clock.
"Roger that," Jack replied.

Above them, the Rover hovered fifteen feet up, its beam piercing the murky gloom. Around them, a kaleidoscope of tropical fish darted past in vibrant flashes — a fleeting burst of color in the deep blue. Mesmerized, Breanna and Jack looked up at the towering port hull looming overhead as they neared the stern. Jack surged ahead behind the galleon, approaching the edge of a sudden, terrifying drop-off.
"About twenty feet to the ravine," he whispered, barely audible.
A cold, sharp stab of fear cut through Breanna. She shivered as the vastness of the ocean seemed to press down on her.
Jack quickly returned to the port side, taking point as they began ascending toward the main deck, shrouded in sand and hidden secrets. They moved across the deck, passing a large jagged hole near the main mast — a dark maw hinting at the wreck's violent end. Breanna glanced at her iPad.
"Time to go," she said firmly, though a tremor betrayed the urgency beneath her calm.
Without hesitation, Breanna surged toward the surface, propelled by a sudden urgency. Jack lingered a moment longer, eyes fixed on the wreck, a fierce determination burning within them, before he too slipped into the green depths and vanished.

A breathtaking sunset spread across the St.Augustine Intracoastal, the sky ablaze with vivid colors. Crimson bled seamlessly into gold, then darkened into a bruised purple at the horizon—a stunning canvas for the unfolding tension.

Tom's F-150 stood alone in the municipal marina parking lot, a solitary sentinel among three patrol cars. Against the dimming sky, Tom and his three deputies formed a grim tableau, each clutching shotguns with a casual yet threatening air. In Tom's hand, a tablet glowed softly, casting light on the photograph of Romer Treese displayed on the "A-7-S Secure Solution" website. The bold letters beneath the image—CHIEF OF SECURITY—stood out sharply against the screen's glow.

"Let's start with this," Tom said quietly, his voice heavy with unspoken menace. "Sea Wench Marine Salvage? A pathetic front. Nothing but pure, unadulterated deception." He paused, letting the weight of his words settle. "Romer Treese. Stanford—*summa cum laude* in Philosophy and English Lit. Ten years in the Navy. Decorated veteran, they say. Now working for A-7-S, a global security firm… with a disturbing taste for the darker side of business." Tom's tone grew harder. "According to the FBI, Treese and his crew are mercenaries. Their résumé? Drug smuggling, arms dealing, and maritime piracy. A trifecta of villainy."

Farther down the marina, the *Orca*'s dark hull shimmered faintly in the dying light, its reflection rippling across the water in languid waves. The surface barely stirred, masking the quiet rhythm of something unfolding beneath.

Below, a lone figure cut through the water with the silent precision of a predator. The scuba diver moved with practiced control—no wasted motion, no hesitation. He reached the underside of the *Orca's* port side and, with deft fingers, secured a small GPS tracker against the hull. A green light blinked to life, subtle and defiant—a silent beacon of resistance, or perhaps a challenge issued in shadow.

As the diver retreated into the dark, a fleeting image caught in the flicker of light: Davis. His face, set and grim behind the curve of his mask, emerged for only a moment. Just long enough to glimpse the man behind the mission.

Tom tucked the tablet under his arm, the fiery hues of the sunset catching in his eyes like embers. Something shifted in his stance—subtle, barely noticeable, but unmistakably strategic. He wasn't just standing there anymore; he was calculating.

"He's probably too smart to have anything blatantly illegal on board," he muttered, mostly to himself, though the deputies nearby caught every word.

"This little wake-up call… is just to let him know we know."

The threat—unspoken, but thick with meaning—hung in the air like a gathering storm.

Aboard the *The Sea Wench*, Romer Treese sat in the cabin, wreathed in the curling haze of cigar smoke. the glow of his laptop bathed his face in pale blue light, a stark contrast to the shadows closing in around him. Onscreen, a Google search blinked: *Sunken ships – St. Augustine.* The room smelled of moneyed indulgence—rich tobacco, leather, and something less identifiable, something tight-coiled and electric.

"Romer! Romer Treese!"

Tom's voice sliced through the night like broken glass—sharp, sudden, impossible to ignore.

Treese's eyes snapped upward, flint-hard and narrowed. Irritation flickered, then quickly ignited into something colder, more dangerous. In a motion so fluid it was almost elegant, he reached beneath the desk and drew a pistol. Heavy. Polished. Lethal. It glinted in the lamplight like a whispered promise. He stormed onto the deck, a thundercloud in motion, fury radiating from every controlled step.

Tom met him on the dock ramp, climbing slowly, steadily. No weapons raised. Just that measured, relentless walk. Treese intercepted him halfway, trailing cigar ash with a flick of his fingers—a lazy, contemptuous flourish meant to provoke.

"What do you want, Sheriff?" His voice was low, a dangerous murmur laced with quiet threat.

Tom held up a crumpled sheet of paper. A search warrant. The wind caught its edge, making it tremble faintly in his grasp.

"I have a warrant to search this ship."

Treese snatched the document without ceremony, scanning it with deliberate, predatory slowness. A smile tugged at the corners of his mouth—thin, mocking, and gone before it settled.

"Is that a fact?"

A long beat passed. Silence spread between them, brittle and electric. Then something shifted behind Treese's eyes. The smug superiority melted, replaced by something cooler, more calculated. Charm, weaponized.

He tucked the pistol just out of sight and took a step back.

"I'm coming aboard now, son. We're not gonna have any problems, are we?"

His gaze swept past Tom, lingering on the deputies at the edge of the dock. Their shotguns gleamed beneath the last light of day, each of them motionless but ready. Treese's smile stretched wider—too wide. A grotesque parody of hospitality.

"Welcome aboard."

The words were hollow. A brittle veneer over the crackling tension that pulsed between the men. It wasn't a greeting. It was a warning. A line drawn. And neither man intended to step back.

Across the marina, the old bridge let out a low, groaning sigh beneath Jack's slow, uncertain steps. The night pressed in all around him—vast, star-strewn, and eerily still. Ahead, Breanna stood at the edge of the walkway, her silhouette small and delicate against the sprawl of constellations above. She didn't turn at his approach, but something in her posture shifted, sensing him, bracing.

The silence between them felt immense. He could hear the distant water lapping against the dock pilings, could feel the unspoken weight that hung in the cool air like mist.

"How are you and Will—" she began, her voice barely more than breath, a fragile sound lost in the enormity of the sky.

Jack stopped. His reply came fast, too sharp.

"Really? Don't open that box. Not now."

His words cut through the stillness like a blade, and she flinched. Just barely. The starlight caught the tremor in her hand as it curled slightly at her side.

"We've gotta go back down there," he said after a moment, voice low but laced with something urgent—desperation, maybe. "Search the wreck."

Breanna turned, the faintest shake of her head betraying her fear.

"Jack, I don't know. If there's a methane hydrate bed at the bottom of that ravine... we just don't have enough data—" Her voice faltered, caught between science and dread.

Jack stared at her, disbelief etched deep into his face. The stars cast his features in pale relief—tight jaw, furrowed brow, the raw edge of frustration.

"Now you wanna be cautious?" he said bitterly. He shook his head, the motion filled with exhausted disbelief. "Why did you even come back?"

"I told you," she said softly. "Will asked me to help and—look, I'm here now."

Her voice was small. It barely rose above the night sounds, almost lost in the wide, endless dark.

Jack looked away. His hands flexed at his sides, his thoughts spinning too fast. The air felt tighter by the second. Breanna waited, her shoulders stiff, her breath shallow.

"Aren't you even a little curious to see what the hell is down there?" he asked suddenly. The question came out rough, like a challenge. Like a dare. Breanna's chest clenched. She stepped forward and wrapped her fingers around the cold railing, gripping it as if to steady herself. Her knuckles blanched white in the starlight.

"We're not treasure hunters, Jack," she said, the words raw with conviction. "We're scientists. This isn't our wheelhouse."

Silence followed, thick and heavy. The kind of silence that says everything.

Below them, the water shifted and sighed, rhythmic and indifferent. The stars blinked overhead, cold witnesses to their impasse.

Then, the slightest movement—Breanna's head tilted, almost imperceptibly. But Jack felt it. Something in him reacted, like a compass needle twitching toward magnetic north. His gaze lifted to meet hers.

Their eyes locked. And for a moment, neither of them spoke. But something passed between them—wordless, weighty, unresolved. A fragile, flickering truce born of shared fear and buried history. A need for meaning in the face of the vast, unknowable dark.

And above them, the stars just kept watching.

Inside the Sea Wench's main cabin, the air was dense, salt-slicked, and tinged with something else. Something harder to name. It clung to the walls, seeped into the threadbare upholstery, coiled in the corners like smoke. Tom moved with quiet deliberation, eyes sharp, body tense. He pressed down on the mattress. It yielded under his touch with a reluctant give, as if trying to withhold secrets long buried in its folds.

He turned to the desk.

Two books sat there, strangely pristine: *Moby Dick*—a title that made him pause. Too fitting. The second, *The Agony and the Ecstasy*, felt like a gut punch. Ironic. Cruel. It mirrored his own inner state far too well.

A shadow seemed to creep into the cabin behind him—not one cast by light, but by something less visible, more insistent. Oppressive. He felt it press against his shoulders like a weight, a presence heavy in the confined space. The hair on his arms prickled. Something in the air whispered caution.

With a sharp breath, Tom turned and climbed out of the hatch. Treese followed silently, too close.

They moved toward the port side, footsteps echoing against the old deck. The ship groaned beneath them, its rhythmic creak filling the silence between the two men like a ticking clock.

"You're wasting everyone's time, Sheriff," Romer muttered. His voice was low, a growl just shy of violence. "Are we… done?"

Tom didn't break stride. "Have a nice night, Romer," he said, his voice clipped and cold.

The words hung for a moment—fragile, brittle, ready to shatter.

Tom descended the ramp with his deputies flanking him, their presence silent but solid. Romer remained behind, a statue in the shadows.

And then it came—the slow curl of a smile. Not warmth, not amusement. This was something else entirely. It unfolded across his face like frost spreading over glass: cold, calculated, and utterly without mercy. A promise unspoken. A reckoning yet to come.

Elsewhere, aboard the *Orca*, Jack entered the lab. The door clicked softly shut behind him.

The room smelled of ozone and stale coffee, the air heavy with long hours and exhausted ambition. He dropped into the chair at the console, its cushions worn and unforgiving. The hush of the late hour pressed in from all sides.

He rubbed his eyes with the heel of one hand, then reached for the keyboard. Fingers sluggish with fatigue hovered, hesitated, then typed.

The monitor flickered to life.

A grainy video filled the screen. He and Breanna stood in the frame, illuminated by the harsh glow of the Galleon's deck lights. Their faces looked younger somehow, despite only days having passed. Brighter. More whole. That moment had been sun-drenched and electric, but the screen cast it in shades of static and shadow.

Now, only the dark watched with him.

Jack leaned back in his chair, shoulders sagging, breath shallow.

The digital clock glared down at him—11:33 p.m.— its red digits pulsing like an unblinking eye.

A long, tired sigh escaped his lips.

Will's voice, low and gravel-thick, sliced clean through the quiet.

"You're up late."

The video cut off with a click, the silence that followed landing with a thud. Jack turned in his chair as his father stepped into the lab, his features lined with wear, his eyes shadowed by something deeper than fatigue.

"Dad—when did you get in?"

"Just now." Will's voice was measured, but beneath it, a tight current of urgency ran. "I needed to talk to you. In person."

Jack offered a weak smile, but it faltered before it could settle. "Whoa. Must be a holiday."

Will didn't respond. He didn't have to.

"This is serious, Jack."

Jack stood slowly, tension knotting in his gut.

"What's going on?"

Behind them, the door creaked open again. Breanna stepped in, eyes wide, uncertainty drawn across her face.

"I'm sorry," she said softly. "I was on the bridge. I saw Will arrive. I can go—"

Will stopped her with a look. "No. Stay. You should hear this too."

Breanna hesitated, then nodded, moving closer.

Will exhaled, the sound as tired as the man himself.

"Raymond pulled the plug. Three days from now, the entire operation runs out of money."

The words hit with the force of a gut punch. Silence followed, thick and suffocating.

"Big Oil strikes again," Jack muttered, though the

bite in his voice couldn't disguise the bitterness underneath.

"They don't want *The Extinction Protocol* released," Will said. The words tasted like defeat.

Breanna's breath caught. "What can we do?"

Will ran a hand over his face. "I'm leaving at first light. Going to try everything—anyone. But Jack, I need you to do the same. Start calling people. Everyone you know. Tell them what we have. Just… tell them the truth."

Jack didn't answer right away. He looked at Breanna—she met his eyes with the same silent dread. A shared flicker of fear passed between them, too familiar now to startle.

"Maybe there's another way," Jack said finally, a faint light kindling behind his words.

Will's expression hardened. "You cutting me a check?"

Jack hesitated, then took a step forward. "We found a shipwreck. A galleon, about forty miles southeast. We haven't fully explored it yet, but Breanna and I were down there today. There's something—there's a real possibility—"

"No." Will shut it down with a sharp wave of his hand. "Stop. I don't have time for treasure hunts or pipe dreams. Are you going to make the calls or not?"

Jack stood still, the weight of disappointment settling over him like dust. "Whatever you need," he murmured.

Will turned to go, then paused at the doorway, his voice quieter. "Is the methane study done?"

Jack winced. "Give me another day or two."
Will's silence said more than words. His disappointment lingered even as he disappeared down the corridor.
"Dad…" Jack called softly. "I'll get the money."
Will paused, half-turned, gave a weary smile, then vanished into the dark.
Breanna approached, her steps slow. She reached out, brushing Jack's shoulder with gentle fingers.
"Calling anyone is useless," she said. The words were soft. Final.
"I know." Jack's voice was little more than a breath.
A beat of quiet passed between them, the kind that stretched longer than it should.
Breanna tilted her head. "If you still want to go… I'm in."
He looked at her. "You sure?"
She hesitated. "Are you?"
He didn't answer right away. Then: "Crew meeting in the galley. Twenty minutes."
Breanna nodded. No more words. She slipped out, leaving Jack alone with the cold hum of the lab.
He sat, the silence around him now somehow louder. The screen flickered to life once more under his touch. His fingers flew across the keyboard, purposefully now. Determined. He clicked through files, opening one after another, until he found what he was looking for.
The glow of the monitor cast long shadows across his face as he leaned in, studying the data like it might save them.
Or bury them deeper.

Global Warming

The glow from Jack's monitor lit the dim cabin with a sterile, unforgiving light. Across the screen, the top Google search results for *Methane – Global Warming* stared back at him with clinical menace.

"SCIENTISTS WARN OF RISING OCEANS AS ANTARCTIC ICE MELTS."

The words loomed like a gathering storm, factual but steeped in silent dread.

"ICE-FREE ARCTIC IN TWO YEARS HERALDS METHANE CATASTROPHE."

A bold prediction. Urgent. Cold. The kind of sentence that didn't need imagery to feel apocalyptic.

"CATASTROPHIC METHANE RELEASE FROM THE THAWING ARCTIC COULD COST THE WORLD OVER $60 TRILLION."

The number alone hit him like a fist. Not just global. Existential.

Jack sat frozen, the stark headlines burning into his brain. His cursor hovered over the first article. He hesitated—just a second—but it was enough to feel the weight of the world balancing on that tiny, blinking arrow. Then he clicked.

The article loaded slowly. Paragraphs slid into place like falling debris, and he began to read, the words blurring around the edges as his focus narrowed. Somewhere deep inside, a cold, leaden dread was settling into his chest. Not panic. Not even fear. Something heavier. Inevitable.

Outside, Will descended the ramp of the *Orca* like a man unraveling. Every step was slow, labored, as if the dock beneath him resisted his weight. The salt air, once familiar and steadying, now tasted metallic—tainted.

"Will." He turned at the sound of her voice, already knowing who it was. Breanna was hurrying toward him, her movements strained, brittle with emotion. Her face was drawn, her eyes rimmed with shadows. She looked like someone carrying too many truths at once.

"We need to talk," she said, and though her voice was soft, it cracked under the pressure.

Will didn't answer at first. He closed his eyes briefly and ran a hand over his face.

"I'm wiped, Breanna. Can it wait?"

"It's already waited too long," she said.

He opened his mouth to argue, then stopped. The look on her face stilled him.

For a moment, neither of them spoke. The dock creaked under their feet, and the hush of the sea filled the silence.

Then Breanna spoke, her voice low and hoarse.

"I pushed Jack to let Billy and Malcolm dive past three thousand." Will didn't react. Not immediately. Just listened.

"He didn't want to. He said it was risky. But I kept pushing. I told him we didn't have time to play it safe. And when it went bad—when we lost them— he took the fall." Will's jaw tensed. "But the blame's mine. Billy and Malcolm are dead because of me."

Her words came slowly, but they landed like falling

bricks. Breanna's breath hitched. Her hand tremble. Will stared at her, the weight of confession dragging every line of his face downward. Guilt radiated from him like heat.

A silence fell between them—thick, leaden, impossible to carry or set down. Neither moved. Neither could.

Inside the *Orca*'s galley, the clatter of forks and knives against ceramic plates sounded sharper than usual—metallic strikes that seemed to echo off the tight walls and bounce around the room like warnings.

Sam sat stiffly, chewing without tasting, his eyes flicking toward the galley entrance every few seconds. Bobbi picked at her food, the tines of her fork scratching faint lines into the rim of her plate. Chip, usually the first to crack a joke or fill the silence with idle chatter, sat mute, his shoulders hunched as though bracing for impact.

The humid air felt almost wet against their skin, the scent of reheated rations doing nothing to ease the queasy stillness. Their conversation—what little there was—was forced, each attempt at normalcy fraying at the edges before it landed.

They weren't waiting for the meal.

They were waiting for something else.

Outside the galley, the sound of Greg's pacing echoed down the narrow corridor, each footfall a sharp, impatient punctuation mark in the uneasy silence. The door shuddered with every pass, a subtle tremor that seeped into the already-tense air within.

Then Breanna appeared.

She stood frozen in the corridor, her face pale, her eyes wide with the unmistakable look of dread. The moment she entered Greg's orbit, she seemed to shrink, as if his presence consumed the hallway itself. His tall frame loomed over her, casting a long shadow that swallowed what little light remained.

"You've been avoiding me, Bree," he said, his voice low and oily, a predator's purr laced with something far more dangerous.

"Greg, please. Not now," she whispered, her voice shaking.

"I know you said we're done," he murmured, his hand sliding across her shoulder in a slow, possessive gesture. "But you never said *why*." He leaned in, his breath brushing her ear. "I'm thinking maybe you changed your mind."

The galley door slammed open.

Jack stood in the threshold, his expression a mixture of disbelief and rage. "What the *hell* is this?" he shouted, the words ripping through the charged air like a lightning strike.

Both Breanna and Greg turned, caught in the spotlight of exposure. Greg's initial confusion flickered across his face before it hardened into a mask of forced calm.

"Jack, wait—" he started.

"*Wait?*" Jack's voice rose, quivering with fury.

Greg tried to wave it off, his tone flat and defensive. "Relax, man. She's a friend. We... we hooked up. Back in Miami."

The silence that followed was unbearable.

Jack's head jerked toward Breanna, eyes wild with betrayal, then snapped back to Greg. His voice dropped to a guttural growl. "You hooked up. With *my ex*. In Miami?"

Greg blinked. "Your ex?" he repeated, feigning ignorance—a weak shield against the storm brewing in Jack's eyes.

"Jack, please listen," Breanna pleaded, stepping forward. "It wasn't—" Her voice cracked.

But Jack wasn't listening. He was already moving. "You're dead!" he snarled, launching himself at Greg. His fist cut through the air like a bullet.

"No!" Breanna screamed.

Greg barely dodged the punch, stumbling backward, then lunged forward, wrapping his arms around Jack in a desperate attempt to restrain him. The two men slammed into the wall, grappling violently, a collision of fists, elbows, and rage. Breanna tried to push between them, crying out, her voice drowned in the chaos.

"You're done!" Jack shouted, struggling harder.

"Chill out, bro! Chill out!" Greg gasped, but his words meant nothing now.

The noise drew the others. Sam, Bobbi, and Chip burst in, galvanized by the shouting. They threw themselves into the fray, dragging Jack back, shouting his name. Bobbi's voice cut through the din. "Boss! That's enough! Let it go!"

Freed from Greg's grip, Jack ripped away from his crew's restraining hands. He stared at Breanna, his breath ragged, his face twisted with heartbreak and disbelief.

"I'm sorry, Jack!" she cried. "Greg and I... it was over before it started."

Jack turned toward Greg, his eyes narrowing, his body trembling with restraint. His gaze swept over the stunned faces in the galley.

"Everybody. Get. In. The. Galley. Now."

His voice was quiet, but each word struck like a hammer. No one dared disobey.

Moments later, the group had assembled. Jack paced at the head of the table, his shadow stretching and curling across the walls like smoke. His eyes never left Breanna.

"The wreck," he said finally, "is twenty feet from a ravine. We think it's sitting on a methane hydrate bed. If we're wrong, this dive is suicide. We could come up with nothing. Or..." He paused, letting the weight of the silence carry the thought.

"...or we could find—"

"*Mucho mucho dinero!*" Chip blurted out with forced enthusiasm, trying to pierce the tension. The attempt fell flat. Greg and Breanna exchanged uneasy glances. Everyone was thinking the same thing: was it worth it?

Jack's gaze was unflinching. "All I promise is this: if we ID the wreck, whatever we bring up, we share. Equally."

Sam leaned toward Bobbi, his voice barely above a whisper. "I've got a bad feeling about this, Cap."

Bobbi gave a dry snort in response, just as Greg chuckled under his breath. But the sound didn't go unnoticed.

"What's so funny, Greg?" she snapped, sharp as a whip.

Greg's smirk faded. "You ever do any dives in South Central, Bobbi? No? Didn't think so."

Sam bristled. "Watch your tone, jerk."

Greg shrugged, a flicker of defiance in his eyes, but said nothing more.

Jack raised his voice again. "It's a galleon, people. A Spanish Galleon. My money's on gold. We'll need double tanks, massive salvage bags—the works. And listen carefully," his tone darkened, "we have to find something that identifies the wreck. That's the law. Otherwise, it's just treasure-hunting. Illegal."

A beat of silence followed. Even the humming of the equipment felt loud.

"Cap," Sam said finally, straightening. "Two words: we're in."

Chip swallowed hard. "We'll need real-time data on that methane hydrate bed. I'll monitor it, keep updates flowing." He looked to Jack, who gave him a nod, the only sign of approval he offered.

"One more thing," Jack added, lowering his voice. "My dad's investors? They've pulled the plug. We've got three days. That's it. Three days to make this pay off, or we're finished."

The room fell quiet. No one argued. No one moved. Tomorrow, the real danger would begin.

The crew began to disperse, their faces marked by a volatile mix of anticipation and dread. No one spoke much—just a few muttered words, uneasy glances, nervous fidgeting as they filtered out into the corridor.

Breanna remained seated.

Her shoulders sagged, her hands limp in her lap, her face drawn and pale. She looked as though she hadn't taken a full breath in minutes. The weight of the moment, of everything that had just unfolded, pressed down on her like the sea itself.

At the door, Greg hesitated.

One foot stepped into the hallway, then stopped. He turned back toward Jack. His face was unreadable—strangely serene, like someone preparing to dive into deep water.

"Listen, bro," Greg said quietly, his voice steady. "We gotta talk."

Jack didn't move. His jaw clenched. "Get out," he growled.

"I swear, Jack—" Greg took a step closer, hands open, voice softening into something that sounded dangerously close to sincere. "Don't make this a mission. I respect you, bro. I don't want trouble."

His eyes met Jack's and held. "Please."

A long silence. The air in the room tightened like a stretched wire.

Jack's glare didn't waver, but something shifted behind his eyes—calculation, perhaps, or just the strain of holding back everything he wanted to say.

"We'll settle this later," he muttered. The words were clipped, sharp enough to cut.

Greg nodded slowly, a flicker of something—relief? amusement? tugging at the corner of his mouth. Jack caught the expression and looked at Breanna, who mirrored his confusion with a furrowed brow.

"What?!" Jack snapped, voice rising again.

Greg didn't flinch. "You said, 'if we can identify the wreck'..." His tone was almost gentle. "I might be able to help you with that."
For a heartbeat, silence claimed the room again, dense and suffocating.

A blast tore through the stillness. The hatch burst open, the sound ricocheting off the dock like a gunshot.
Jack and Greg emerged from the belly of the Orca, surging into the night with frantic urgency. They walked side by side across the dock, boots echoing against the planks, their figures swallowed quickly by the dark.
"How the hell can you help with this?" Jack shouted, his voice broke with disbelief.
Greg didn't slow. He didn't even glance over.
"You'll see," he said, calmly—too calmly.
Jack stumbled for half a second, shaken by the quiet certainty in Greg's reply, before pushing harder into his stride. The shadows seemed to chase them down the dock, long fingers reaching, stretching toward the marina parking lot ahead.

The salt-laced wind whipped through Treese's hair as he and Davis stood on the deck. The stubs of their cigars glowed like malevolent embers, flickering defiantly against the swallowing darkness. Below them, the figures of Jack and Greg vanished into the inky night, swallowed whole by shadows. A furious, muttered curse drifted up from the dock, trailing behind them like a warning.
"So," Davis purred, his voice low and rough, blending

with the rhythm of the rising tide, "how did my little night swim work out?"

Treese pulled the GPS receiver from his pocket—a cold, metallic weight in his hand. With a slow, deliberate press of a button, a smile curled across his lips—sharp and chilling. Davis's eyes flicked to the digital display:
29.89° N – 81.31° W. The numbers burned into the darkness like a brand.
"Great," Davis rasped, suspicion tightening his tone. "But why do we care?"
Treese's gaze locked on the retreating figures, their frantic pace caught in the glow of distant city lights. A dark, predatory gleam kindled in his eyes.
"A hunch," he hissed, venom dripping from the word. "A damnable hunch that those two idiots are onto something big. Follow them, Davis. Find out what they're digging up before they bury it... permanently."
Without a word, Davis flicked his cigar stub away with a casual wrist and slipped into the shadows, moving with the quiet efficiency of a hunter. Treese watched him disappear, a low, guttural chuckle rumbling in his chest—a sound as cold and dark as the ocean itself.
The night held its breath.
The game had begun.

The Bell

Hector sat on the front porch, an easel before him and a canvas half-covered with swirling strokes of paint. Brushes and tubes lay scattered haphazardly across the weathered wooden floorboards. The sharp scent of turpentine hung heavy in the humid air, mingling with the salty tang of the ocean breeze drifting in from the nearby shore. He worked steadily, brow furrowed in deep concentration, glancing up now and then at the full moon. Its silver light cast a gentle glow over the subtle texture of his painting — a turbulent sea under the rising moon, darkened by the silhouette of a lone ship's mast. The crunch of footsteps on gravel drew Hector's attention. Greg and Jack were approaching, climbing the creaky porch steps. Greg threw an arm around Hector in a warm, bear-like hug.

"Abuelo, you remember Jack," Greg rumbled softly. Jack extended his hand with a respectful nod. "Mr. Sandoval. How are you, sir?"

Hector smiled, the fine lines around his eyes deepening with age and kindness, then returned to his work. "As good as an old man can be," he murmured, his voice rough like the sea-worn wood beneath them.

Greg stepped closer, eyeing the painting with interest. "Ah, something different. Bueno, bueno." He pointed out the faint shimmer embedded in the paint—tiny specks of sand or shell, catching the moonlight just so.

Hector set down his brush carefully, a flicker of something unreadable passing through his gaze. His usually stoic expression softened just a fraction, revealing a hint of anticipation. "So, have you been down to the wreck?" His tone dropped low, serious. "Yes, we have," Greg replied, sharing a meaningful glance with Jack.

A battered black pickup truck rolled slowly past the house, its paint faded and chipped. Davis sat behind the wheel, casting a sharp look toward the porch before driving on. Hector's eyes narrowed as he followed the truck's progress, his posture stiffening with quiet alertness. The glint in his gaze sharpened. "Let's go inside," Hector said, his voice firm.
He led them into the dim, salt-scented house, where the air hung thick with the smell of old wood and sea breeze. Greg flicked on a light switch, revealing dusty furniture and faded photographs hanging crookedly on the walls. Jack followed Hector into the dining room, his eyes catching on a collection of nautical charts and weathered maps pinned up, their faded annotations still decipherable. Hector opened a closet door, revealing a narrow, concealed staircase descending into shadow.
"Gregory?" Hector's voice dropped to a whisper. Greg's attention was caught by an old wooden box on the floor, its lid cracked open to reveal a tarnished brass bell nestled inside. He grunted softly as he lifted it onto the table. The bell was intricately engraved with swirling patterns, and an inscription faint but still legible.

Jack leaned in, fingers tracing the corroded metal. The name "Arabelle" stood out clearly.

"Arabelle," Jack muttered. "Why do I know that name?"

Hector leaned closer, resting a surprisingly gentle hand on Jack's shoulder. His voice dropped to a conspiratorial murmur. "Young man, what year was the Castillo de San Marcos completed?"

Jack frowned, searching his memory. "Sometime in the 1690s?"

"1695," Hector confirmed, a faint smile tugging at his lips. But it didn't reach his eyes — those carried the weight of decades, heavy with secrets and unspoken knowledge about the treasure hidden within that old bell. Unnoticed, Davis crept toward the side of the house, ducking under a shutter to peer through an open window. His shadowed anticipation mirrored that of the old man inside.

"The fort was built to defend St. Augustine," Hector's voice was low, resonant, "but also to honor a lost galleon and its lone surviving sailor—whose wish was that the *Arabelle* never be forgotten. It stayed there until one summer night in 1923... when it simply disappeared."

Greg laid a hand on the bell, its cool metal stark against the humid Florida air. "My great-grandfather, Professor Elias Sandoval, meticulously documented local lore. His journals are filled with sketches, transcribed legends, and what we now know are detailed analyses of the *Arabelle's* navigational charts — charts that back up Carlos Sandoval's incredible story of survival."

Jack's eyes darted between Greg and Hector, disbelief and fascination etched deep on his face. "You're saying," he said slowly, "he stole the bell?"

"We prefer 'reclaimed,'" Hector replied with a twinkle in his eye.

Greg leaned forward. "A year after the *Arabelle* went down, Carlos returned to Spain a hero. He was named 'Special Envoy' by King Philip and Queen Mariana — the royal's eyes and ears in Florida. Between 1671 and 1695, he oversaw seven governors during the fort's construction. But his reports... they're cryptic."

Hector shuffled to a chair, tapping his cane nervously on the floor. Jack stared at Greg, torn between skepticism and growing excitement.

"Sounds like you did your homework," Jack admitted, impressed despite himself.

Greg glanced at Hector. "Bro, you have no idea." He sipped water, the tension thickening the room.

"We are Sandoval," Hector declared, voice stronger than before. "Whatever treasure is on that ship is rightfully ours."

"Abuelo, please," one of Hector's grandsons began. Hector slammed his cane down, silencing him. "Yes, we do! How many wrecks did I dive with my father? How many did you dive with me, chasing this needle in a haystack? I always knew they weren't *Arabelle*... just like I know now. I can feel it."

Davis pressed his back against the house, eyes wide like saucers. "No freakin' way, man!," he whispered, stunned.

"We still have to ID the wreck definitively," Jack said, anticipation rising in his voice. "And if you're right, you're holding the proof."

"I will continue to," Hector affirmed, eyes gleaming. "Until the time is right."

Suddenly energized, Davis slipped away from the house, then bolted. His escape was a blur.

Jack's gaze lingered on the bell, its ornate carvings whispering forgotten history. "Mr. Sandoval, maybe we should take the bell. It'll be safer with us."

"How could it possibly be safer?" Hector challenged, unwavering.

Jack's impassive stare met Hector's. He knew the truth — the real danger wasn't thieves, but those who already knew about the treasure and wanted it for themselves.

Davis sped away, phone pressed to his ear.

"701 Galiano Street. I'll wait around the corner." He ended the call, barely containing his glee. The sound of his speeding car faded into the night, leaving a silent, tense agreement hanging in the air.

Greg hurried to the Jeep, carrying the old box with Jack close behind. He placed it on the back seat.

Jack's eyes flashed with jealousy as they climbed in. Jack stuck the key in the ignition. The engine coughed, sputtered, then roared to life — a sound matching the tension thickening the air.

"How long have you known about this?"

Jack's voice tightened.

"My grandfather first showed me the bell when I was five. Made me swear never to tell," Greg said steadily, though a tremor quivered in his hands. "Now, the Sandoval three-century obsession is in your back seat. I'm in the game with you, bro. Comprende? And if you and Bree aren't tight, it's got nothing to do with me."

Jack's knuckles whitened on the wheel. He slammed the car into gear, accelerating too fast, almost violently.

Greg's jaw tightened. The box's weight in the backseat suddenly felt heavier, oppressive. He glanced back toward the house, catching a flicker of movement — a dark figure silhouetted in the window, watching. The figure raised a hand, a gesture both warning and invitation.

Jack swallowed hard. The evening's weight pressed down on him. Their journey had just begun, and the stakes were higher than he ever imagined.

Hector stood before his easel, the moonrise painting a cruelly serene backdrop to the terror swelling in his chest. Violent pounding at the door startled him.

"Gregory? BAM! BAM! BAM! BAM!"

"Just a minute!" Hector rasped, voice trembling. He gripped his cane tightly, each shuffle slow and frail. The door burst open, revealing Treese and Davis — masked, guns drawn, muzzles mere inches from his temple. Cold steel bit into his aging skin.

"Step back, Abuelo," Treese snarled, venom dripping from every word.

Defiance flickered in Hector's eyes, but his body
betrayed him. He tried to stand firm, but age and
fear weighed heavy, slowing him like chains.
"You've picked the wrong house," he croaked, voice
tight with desperation. "I don't have anything."
Without warning, Davis moved like a storm—brutal
and unstoppable. He shoved Hector aside with a
sickening crack as the old man slammed into the
wall. Davis tore into the dining room, chaos trailing
him—glass shattered, wood splintered, a violent
symphony of destruction.
Treese slammed the door shut behind them, his grip
on Hector's arm ironclad, unyielding. The room
echoed with crashing chairs and exploding boxes, a
maelstrom of havoc.
"Sit!" Treese's voice dropped low, a growl laced with
menace.
Hector's eyes flicked to Davis, who ransacked the
room with the fury of a cornered beast. Treese's
burning gaze pinned Hector, cold and merciless.
"I *said,* sit!" The word hit like a fist.
Hector crumpled into the chair, breath caught in his
throat. Davis stalked forward, savage impatience
contorting his face. He yanked Hector up by the shirt
collar, the fabric tearing beneath the strain.
"Where's the bell?" Davis roared, raw fury barely
contained.
Hector's eyes went wide; fear clawed at his throat.
"Bell? I don't have a doorbell! Isn't that why you
knocked?" he stammered.
Davis raised his hand, ready to strike. Hector
flinched, body convulsing in anticipation of

pain. But Treese shoved Davis back with surprising force.

"Have a little respect," Treese hissed, venom thick in his voice. He leaned close, hot breath washing over Hector's face. "You have something I want. I know you have it. Make this easy. Tell us where it is, and we'll be gone."

"There's no bell here!" Hector gasped, voice strangled and fragile.

Treese straightened, eyes burning through Hector's soul. He glanced at Davis, then stepped back. Before Hector could react, Davis's open palm cracked brutally into his face. Hector's head snapped back, colliding with the coffee table in a sickening crunch. He collapsed to the floor—a broken heap of bone and blood.

"It's here," Treese whispered, low and satisfied, the promise of dark triumph curling his words. "I can feel it."

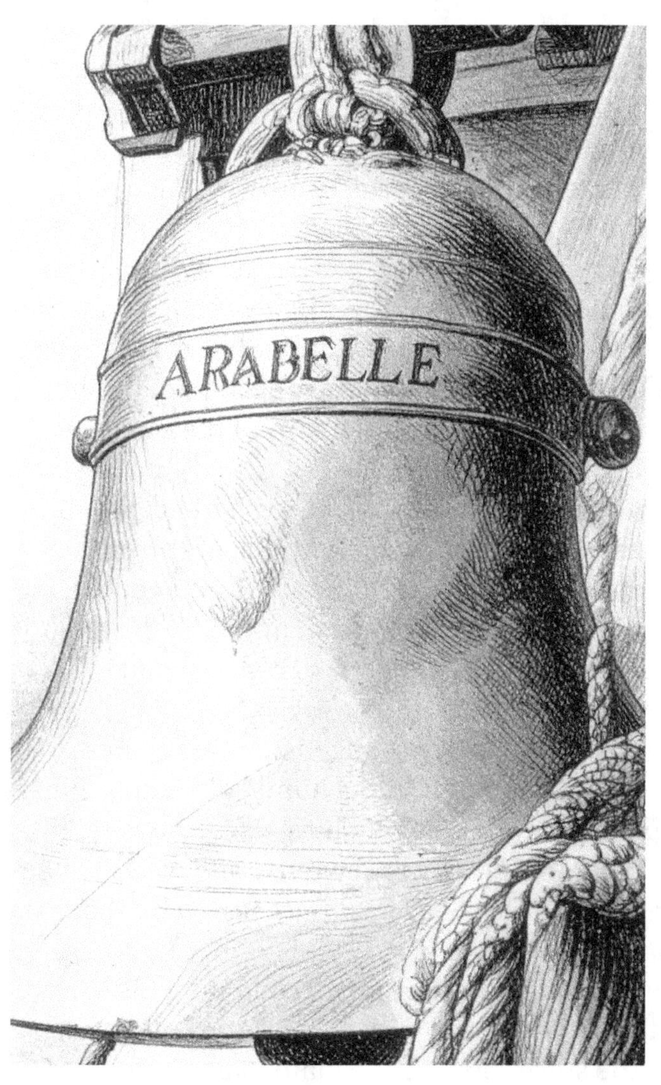
ARABELLE

Proof Of Origin

The Orca sat anchored, steadfast against the vast, sun-drenched Atlantic. God's own spotlight—the morning sun—pierced through the crystalline water, fracturing the surface into a cascade of shimmering diamonds.

Jack's gaze sliced the horizon like a hawk's, sharp and unyielding. Nearby, Breanna wrestled with the heavy weight of her double tanks, her eyes as sharp and lethal as the dive knife strapped to her thigh, steady under the watchful hands of the ever-efficient Sam and Bobbi.

"Fifty-cubic-foot side tanks," Greg barked, his voice roughened by years of salt and sun, gesturing toward the polished equipment. "Brand new salvage bags, too. We're not losing a damn thing this time." His eyes held a mix of paternal concern and unwavering resolve.

Breanna and Bobbi exchanged nervous glances, the pressure coiling tight in the humid air. Sam's fingers snapped Breanna's helmet into place, the metallic clang echoing sharply in the tense silence. Breanna caught Jack's eye — a silent pact sealed by shared danger.

Greg hovered over the sonar readout on his battered iPad, leaning close to Jack. "Check the belfry. It'll be near the stern, close to the main mast. Any treasure's going to be in the lower decks — captain's quarters, most likely. Find anything that identifies the ship — a bell, a crest, whatever..."

He paused, a knowing smirk twitching at his lips. "Got it?"

Jack leaned toward Breanna, his voice low. "Let's go. No talking. Eyes open."

Without hesitation, Jack became a streak of motion, plunging into the turquoise depths. Breanna followed, adrenaline eclipsing her doubts, a fleeting, pained smile for Bobbi.

Seven miles north, a sleek gray GO-FAST boat sliced through the glassy waters, its engine as silent and deadly as a viper stalking prey. Treese's face was carved with a predator's intensity as he peered through his Alpen 853 scope — a military-grade marvel any sniper would envy. Davis gripped the wheel tightly, eyes flicking to the GPS tracker: 29.64 N – 80.66 W. The coordinates seared into his mind. Treese lowered the scope, voice low and certain. "They've got it, Davis. No doubt about it."

Davis let out a grunt. "So, what's the play with this bell?"

Treese chuckled — a low, guttural sound that promised trouble. "Proof of origin. Doubles, maybe triples, the treasure's worth." He pulled two hand-rolled Cuban cigars from his pocket, the scent rich and intoxicating. "If they find anything, let them do the heavy lifting. My cut? You and the boys keep it. Consider it a bonus... for your loyalty. Malcolm's been gone a year. Time Jack LaPointe met the hurt locker."

Davis accepted a cigar, a grin spreading wide as the ocean itself. They lit up, smoke curling in the humid air — a quiet toast to the chaos just over the horizon.

Sunlight fractured and shimmered, scattering across the surface as Jack and Breanna propelled themselves with powerful dolphin kicks through the cerulean depths. Above them, Rover—the submersible drone—hovered like a metallic manta ray, its single camera eye a watchful cyclops. Around them, a kaleidoscope of iridescent tropical fish—parrotfish glowing like molten sunsets, angel fish shimmering like floating jewels—darted obliviously, untouched by the drama unfolding below.
"Tiger shark, ten o'clock, Jack," Breanna's voice cut crisp and urgent over the comms. A sleek gray torpedo of a shark trailed a frenzied school of jacks, their scales flickering like spilled mercury just to port of the galleon. Another mirrored predator stalked close behind. A deadly ballet in the turquoise deep.
"How you doin', Chip?" Jack's response was terse, focus sharpened like a blade. The comms crackled to life. "About to shed some light on the subject," Chip's voice rasped through static.
Ignoring the interference, Jack's grim face hardened. Breanna's lips twitched with a ghost of a smirk as she nudged him toward the galleon's skeletal remains. The wreck's timbers, encrusted with coral and alive with marine creatures, loomed in the gloom. Their dive lights sliced through the murk, revealing a narrow, shadowed passage barely wide enough to squeeze through. Their tanks hissed softly

— the adventure was only beginning. Centuries-old secrets swirled in the water around them.

Above the ravaged deck, Rover hovered twenty feet up, its powerful lights cutting through the dark, turning the scene into a ghostly underwater tableau. Breanna's dive mask reflected the eerie glow as she followed Jack toward the ship's shattered stern.

"I'm heading for the belfry," Jack announced, voice muffled by his comms unit. The belfry — or what was left of it — jutted like a broken tooth from the shattered superstructure. Rover drifted closer, its mechanical hum a subtle counterpoint to the ocean's muffled roar.

Breanna picked up a corroded metal hook and mounting bracket from the debris-strewn deck.

"This must have been the mount," she murmured.

"But the bell's long gone." Jack fought to mask his barely-contained excitement.

"Chip, I'm going to access the lower deck where the main mast went down," he reported into his comm. They slinked across the deck, past a cabin door hanging on a single hinge, revealing a dark, watery abyss within. Rover hovered above as they reached a gaping hole — a yawning maw in the ship's midsection, swallowing all light.

Jack plunged through without hesitation, swallowed by ink-black water. Breanna followed a beat later, heart pounding a wild rhythm.

"I'm going in," she announced, voice tight with anticipation.

"Right behind you," Chip's voice crackled through the comm.

Rover glided silently behind, its lights casting an eerie, ethereal glow over the vast lower deck. Ancient cannons stood like silent sentinels, their muzzles yawning wide, skeletal jaws frozen in time. Cannonballs lay scattered across the silt-covered planks, like macabre marbles resting beneath the weight of centuries. As they moved deeper, the water grew murkier, the silt swirling around them like a ghostly shroud.

"Check the cannons for any markings that could identify the ship," Jack ordered, his voice calm but sharp.

"I thought we weren't talking," Breanna shot back, a playful edge hiding beneath her words.

"We're not," Jack replied with a grin, the humor crackling faintly through the comms.

Breanna kicked toward the nearest cannon, sweeping away layers of silt with practiced precision. Rover hovered above, its pinpoint beams slicing through the gloom. Chip, monitoring the feed from his iPad, watched intently on the surface. Breanna slipped between the cannon barrels—then recoiled sharply, a gasp escaping her lips. Even through the murky water, the sight was bone-chilling.

On Chip's screen, a human skeleton lay trapped beneath the cannon's barrel, a pale eel writhing as it slithered from the skull's empty eye socket.

"Hope you're enjoying yourself," Jack quipped dryly, amusement in his voice.

Chip's muffled laughter echoed faintly through the silence. Breanna edged away from the grim tableau, muttering under her breath, "Idiot."

Jack swam over, their faces bathed in the drone's steady, unwavering light. Suddenly, a horrific grinding sound shattered the silence—a deep, shuddering groan that seemed to vibrate through the very bones of the sunken ship.

Jack and Breanna locked eyes, fear flickering in their gaze. Endless seconds stretched into eternity before the rumble ceased as suddenly as it had begun.

"What the hell was that?" Breanna gasped, voice tight with tension.

Only the rhythmic hiss of their dive regulators answered.

"Chip, do you copy?" Jack's voice was strained, barely above a whisper.

"Are you guys alright?" Chip's anxious crackle cut through the static.

"No, we're not alright. What just happened?"

"I think that was an earthquake," Chip replied, awe threading through his words. "Must've been an aftershock. Guess my theory's right."

Breanna shot Jack a wide-eyed look, the unspoken question hanging heavy in the thick, waterlogged silence. The adventure had just twisted into something far more dangerous—potentially deadly. Jack, taut as a coiled spring of muscle and adrenaline, surged toward her, his dive fins stirring a miniature vortex in the silt-choked water.

"Let's play it safe and get topside," he grunted, voice barely audible over the ghostly groans of the wounded ship. "Captain's cabin first. Might find something useful there—or at least a decent bottle to celebrate making it out alive."

He blasted upward through the yawning hole in the deck like a human torpedo bursting free of the submerged wreck. Breanna shadowed him closely, their dive lights slicing fleeting beams through the murky gloom. They navigated the debris-strewn main deck, the skeletal vessel creaking and groaning around them like a dying beast.

"I think that quake shifted the whole damn thing," Breanna yelled, voice taut with alarm. "We should get out before it collapses for good!"

Jack ignored her, eyes fixed on a heavy oak door that stubbornly resisted his first attempts to budge it. He gave it a Herculean shove, muscles straining, but the door remained immovable, silent and unyielding. Frustration carved deep lines across his face. He scanned for a latch, a weakness, anything.

"Seriously? Jack, are you listening? This whole place could cave in on us any second!" Breanna's voice cracked with rising panic.

Still unmoved, Jack planted his fins firmly against the deck, braced himself, and let out a guttural grunt as he rammed his shoulder into the door like a battering ram. The ancient wood groaned in protest; a jagged crack spiderwebbed along the frame before the door finally splintered open with a thunderous crack.

He plunged into the cabin, dive light cutting through the stale water and decay, illuminating the scene: a mahogany desk scarred by time and salt, a chart table strewn with rotted navigational maps, and the tattered remains of a once-majestic oak four-poster bed, its grandeur drowned beneath the weight of years.

Suddenly, Rover—their submersible drone—whirred to life, its powerful lamp piercing the cramped quarters with a harsh, focused beam. Breanna, finally closing the gap behind Jack, began her methodical sweep of the desk, her movements sharp and efficient.

But Jack's gaze snagged on something else: a large, iron-bound box tucked beneath the chart table. He wrestled it free, the rusted surface slick with clinging silt. With a grunt, he pried the latch open; the hinges groaned in bitter protest. As the lid creaked back, revealing its hidden contents, his head whipped toward Breanna, eyes wide with disbelief—silent horror spilling from deep inside him.

Salt spray stung Chip's face as he gripped the railing of the Orca, the dive platform groaning under the weight of returning divers. Jack surfaced first, his face pale but resolute beneath a sheen of sweat and seawater. Breanna followed, her usually vibrant dark hair plastered against her skull. She hauled herself aboard with practiced ease, but her ragged breaths betrayed the strain.

Sam and Bobbi, faces etched with anticipation, reached down, their powerful arms hoisting the heavy salvage bag aboard with a grunt.

Jack, climbing onto the platform, ripped off his mask.

The sight that followed was enough to make a grown man weep—or at least shout. As Sam and Bobbi wrestled open the bag, twelve gleaming gold bars, each wrapped in aged canvas, winked in the sunlight, their burnished surfaces reflecting the turbulent turquoise sea.

"Holy Mary, Mother of God!" Sam roared, voice cracked with disbelief. Bobbi's whoop echoed across the water, swallowed almost instantly by the vast ocean's expanse.

Jack's eyes flickered with a dangerous mixture of relief and something darker—grim determination. His calloused hand swept over the cold metal bars; the biting chill a stark contrast to the blazing heat pressing down from above. The gold's glint burned brighter than the afternoon sun.

"Let's get this below, pronto," Jack barked, voice hoarse from the dive, tension coiled tight in his shoulders. Sam and Bobbi, fueled by the find, stowed the dive gear with lightning efficiency. Chip and Greg, moving like a well-oiled machine, shouldered the heavy bag.

Breanna lingered, a nervous smile barely masking the turmoil inside. Her eyes locked with Jack's—a silent conversation crackling in the charged air, a battle of wills compressed into a single, lingering glance. Then, with a subtle nod, she turned and followed Chip and Greg below, leaving Jack alone on the platform, the weight of the gold matched only by the burden of unspoken fears.

Far off, faint against the shimmering horizon, the

sleek lines of Treese's support vessel cut silently through the water. Treese's grim face lowered the high-powered scope, passing it to Davis.

"Time to move," he growled, voice low and menacing. "Stay close to our new 'friends.' I'll handle the rest. One wrong move, and the whole ocean becomes our graveyard."

The Orca's galley pulsed with raw, unleashed energy—like a thousand-horsepower engine roaring to life. Chip, a cyclone of manic excitement, *popped* the cork on a magnum of Dom Pérignon. The champagne erupted in a sparkling geyser, showering the air with fizz and celebration. The crew roared approval, glasses clinking in a chaotic symphony like a thousand tiny cymbals. Even Jack and Breanna— usually statuesque, carved from granite—allowed faint, guarded smiles.

Twelve gleaming gold bars, each roughly the size of a brick, lay spread across the scarred mahogany table, catching and fracturing the flickering light from overhead lamps.

"To Jack—the man about to make us richer than Croesus!" Chip's voice thundered, excitement spilling over like a kid on Christmas morning who just stumbled on buried pirate loot.

Bobbi giggled—a tinkling sound like wind chimes caught in a tropical storm—while Sam let out a whoop that rattled the bulkhead. Greg, ever the cautious one, managed a nervous grin, his eyes darting anxiously like a bird trapped in a cage. Breanna lifted one of the bars, its weight solid and surprising. She rolled it in her hands, inspecting the smooth, unblemished surface.

"How much more you think's down there, Cap?" Bobbi asked, voice low, almost reverent.

"Where there's a little, there's a lot, right, Jack?" Chip added, eyes glittering with greed.

Jack shrugged, his expression unreadable, as fathomless as the ocean depths. "We're gonna find out."

"But we're not exactly equipped for serious treasure recovery, are we?" Breanna's voice held a sharp edge of worry.

Jack swirled the champagne in his glass, his gaze locking onto Sam. "Then we get set up. Tonight."

Greg's voice cracked with anxiety. "But without the ship's ID? Aren't we committing a felony of epic proportions?"

Silence fell, thick and suffocating.

Jack pulled a single ancient gold coin from his pocket, its surface etched with a finely detailed engraving. He shot Greg a knowing look, noticing how Greg's usually sharp, calculating eyes were glued to Breanna instead.

"Found this in the captain's quarters," Jack said, voice low and deliberate. "Philip the Fourth, King of Spain, 1621 to 1665. One coin might hint at origin, but those bars... they're clean as a whistle."

He paused, letting the weight of his words settle like a shroud.

"England and Spain fought over St. Augustine for two hundred years. Maybe this gold was meant to be untraceable. Maybe it was meant to fund a war."

His voice hardened, steel replacing curiosity.
"We need more than one coin. We need a name. Let's go find it."

The others scrambled out of the galley in a flurry of motion and purpose. Greg lingered behind, his usual calm shattered, nerves raw beneath the surface. Breanna glanced back at Jack, a flicker of curiosity sparking in her eyes before she slipped after the others. Jack closed the door behind them—the sharp click echoing in the sudden, heavy silence.
"Abuelo's right," Greg muttered, a grim satisfaction curling his lips. "She's the Arabelle."
"We don't know that," Jack shot back, his voice tight, controlled.
Greg slammed his fist on the table, making the gold bars leap like startled fish. "Look at that coin! Come on—the ship's bell was missing!"
"Not enough," Jack insisted, panic rising beneath his calm. "To make a claim like that, we need absolute"
"Coño, Jack!" Greg snapped, his patience finally breaking, voice rough with frustration.
Jack cut him off with a hard, steely glare. "Absolute proof. And if you want any future on this ship—or in this crew—you'll keep your distance from Breanna."

A Hundred Million Reasons

The next morning, the salt-laced air hung heavy and thick as Greg and Bobbi wrestled crates aboard the Orca. A pneumatic drill screamed—a metallic banshee wail—that shredded the morning's fragile quiet. Sam, a mountain of a man with hands like shovels, secured a ten-foot crane to the pitching deck, the steel beast dwarfing the vessel's bulk. Breanna, her raven hair stark against the dull gray sky, approached Jack. He stood ramrod straight near the bow, eyes fixed on the churning, steel-colored Atlantic.

"I've analyzed yesterday's scans," Breanna said, voice taut with urgency. "The wreck... it moved. Whatever safety margin we had? It's gone. We're talking millimeters, Jack. Millimeters."

Jack absorbed the news with a tightening jaw. The ocean's salty tang couldn't drown out the metallic taste of dread pooling in his mouth. This wasn't a minor shift—it was a tectonic threat waiting to erupt.

"Time to get to work," he muttered, eyes unwavering from the restless sea.

Breanna raised an eyebrow—she'd seen that look before. It spelled trouble and a hell of a lot of overtime. Just then, Tom appeared, striding down the dock with purpose. Jack, sensing a needed distraction, hustled to meet him.

"Hey, Tommy," Jack greeted, slapping him on the back hard enough to rattle teeth.

"Will's pushing you hard," Tom said low.

"Something like that," Jack nodded toward the crane. The steel leviathan loomed over them all.

Tom slipped his arm around Jack's shoulders, pulling him along with a conspiratorial ease. "If you're back in port tonight, meet me at Scarlett's. My treat."

"You're on," Jack replied, a flicker of something— apprehension?—lurking in his voice.

Tom's gaze flicked to the crane, the easy camaraderie suddenly replaced by a sharp chill. He pulled back, arm dropping to his side, voice dropping with warning.

"Whatever you're doing out there," Tom said quietly, "be careful. Really careful."

He headed for his battered Ford pickup, the engine groaning a mournful farewell to the fragile morning calm. Jack watched him go, a knot tightening in his gut. Tom always knew when something was off. Tom climbed into the truck, the worn leather groaning under his weight. Silence filled the cab, broken only by distant gull cries. He reached for his phone, thumb hovering over speed dial. A long pause before the automated voice answered: "Please leave a message after the tone." BEEP.

Tom's voice came out strained and tight, cutting through the stillness. "It's Tom. Hit me up when you get this. It's important."

He ended the call, worry etched deep in his face.

The Orca, a steel leviathan of a research vessel, rested like a slumbering whale in deceptively calm seas. A taut, nervous energy crackled between Jack and Breanna; her usually vibrant eyes narrowed with deep concern. They slapped on their dive helmets—the metallic clang echoing the mounting tension—then plunged into the indigo depths with the practiced grace of seasoned professionals. Above, Chip expertly guided the remotely operated vehicle deeper into the murky abyss, its tether a fragile lifeline to the surface. *Back into the black,* Jack thought grimly.

"Where to today, Captain Jack?" Chip's voice crackled over the comm, a persistent fly buzzing in their ears.

"Give it a rest, will ya, Chip?" Jack growled, his voice muffled by the water but thick with frustration. Chip, bless his clueless heart, didn't grasp the urgency. "One more quake, and we're gonna have to break off the search," he pressed, worry threading his tone.

Silence followed. A suffocating, pressure-building silence gnawed at their nerves more than any tremor.

"Let's try the gun deck first," Jack decided, clipped and cold. "Sonar shows a likely access point to the lower decks there."

More silence, broken only by Breanna's barely suppressed sigh—exasperation bleeding through. Time was running out, and the ocean refused to cooperate.

They neared the gaping hole in the main deck—a jagged wound scarring the ancient warship's hull.

"Chip, you ready for a visual?" Jack called, voice tight.

"Having trouble hearing you," came the crackling reply, static spitting like angry sea spray.

Breanna rolled her eyes—a gesture swallowed by the murky gloom—as they slipped through the breach, disappearing into the ship's shadowy innards.

Ghostly bronze cannons loomed, their barrels thick with centuries of marine growth. Jack and Breanna, twin phantoms in their gear, moved silently through the eerie cathedral of the gun deck. Their powerful dive lights cut through the gloom, scanning the far walls. Ever meticulous, Breanna made a beeline for a corner, her gloved hands probing piles of cannonballs and weathered crates. She heaved aside a few empty boxes, revealing… nothing but shadows. The dark held its secrets close.

The cold seawater slapped against the hull as they sliced through the ink-black depths. Their dive lights—twin blades—cut a path along the submerged deck's length. Reaching the bow, Jack's beam danced like a restless viper, probing every shadow. Breanna's fins stirred a miniature blizzard of silt against the sandy floor. Then—a glint. Not just any glint, but the faint, tantalizing suggestion of a concealed hatch, almost swallowed whole by centuries of sediment.

Jack's instincts—sharpened by years of underwater escapes that would make Sir Francis Drake blush— kicked in instantly. With brutal efficiency, he scraped away sand, his hand uncovering the rusted

metal lip of a hidden portal. A classic concealment—
the kind only a pirate or a cunning naval architect
could devise.
They exchanged a glance—a silent pact of shared
anticipation. Pure Cusslerian treasure-hunting thrill.

Below, Jack's muscles tensed beneath his wetsuit. He
planted his fins, found a grip on the corroded hatch,
and with a grunt of effort, heaved it open. The
massive iron door groaned its protest after decades
of silence, swinging wide to reveal a yawning maw
of shadow leading into the unknown depths.
A quick, nervous glance passed between Jack and
Breanna, then they plunged into the abyss.
The lower deck yawned like a cavernous tomb, thick
with swirling silt—the sediment of centuries. Their
dive lights crisscrossed through the murk, revealing
a scene of decaying grandeur: a long, empty expanse
littered with skeletal barrels, their shattered staves
whispering of a history swallowed by the ocean's
cold, unyielding grasp. Frustration crept into their
expressions.
Then, a sudden flash—fleeting, impossible—a
golden shimmer that made Breanna's pulse leap
before it vanished like a ghost.
"Did you see that?" she breathed.
"What?" Jack snapped, already shifting his focus to
where she pointed.
"There!"
Breanna spun around, gasping. In the darkest corner
of the stern, bathed in their weak, wavering beams,
lay the prize. Stacks of broken crates spilled

gleaming gold bars. Four massive chests, crusted with barnacles and scarred by time, stood like ancient sentinels against the rear bulkhead. The deck itself seemed to glisten with gold, reflecting their lights in a hypnotic, shimmering dance.

They moved forward cautiously, the silence broken only by the rhythmic whoosh of their breathing and the pounding of their hearts. With a decisive WHACK of his dive hammer, Jack shattered a rusted lock. The chest lids creaked open, revealing a breathtaking hoard of gold bars and exquisite jewelry. Breanna's gasp echoed pure awe."Whoa," Jack muttered, his voice a low rumble of disbelief. The silence returned, broken only by the whispering currents—a quiet testament to their incredible find.

"Jack, over here!" Breanna called, her voice barely audible above the ocean's relentless surge, which gnawed hungrily at the wreck's ancient timbers. Jack fought his way through a swirling vortex of silt and debris, the crushing pressure on his lungs a constant reminder of their peril. Together, they heaved at a waterlogged crate; the rusted iron straps groaned under the strain. Cannonballs, bowling ball-sized, tumbled free, narrowly missing Breanna's head. Finally, the last obstacle cleared—a massive, barnacle-encrusted wooden door loomed before them.

"What is wrong with you? What?" Jack's voice cracked sharply as shattered glass in the tight silence. Oh, no. Here it came. "You should've told me," he hissed, eyes blazing with frustration. He yanked at the door handle, the ancient wood splintering under the strain. It swung inward with a mournful groan, revealing not just a stairway plunging into the sunken vessel's bowels, but a chasm of unspoken words.

Jack barely registered the tension. "You waited for it to blow up! You always wait, hoping some miracle will erase your screw-up instead of just telling me the truth!" Breanna's fingers dug into his bicep as they faced off—a frozen tableau of blame framed by the dark, forbidding stairwell. The treasure, the gleaming riches, faded into the background, swallowed by their argument.

"What do you want me to say?!" Breanna's voice cracked—raw, choked with frustration, but laced with something else: desperate hope.

"You're right!"

Back on the Orca, the scene played out on Chip's oversized iPad like an underwater soap opera for the crew. Sam, Bobbi, and Greg watched intently, their faces a mix of morbid fascination and popcorn-munching anticipation.

Suddenly, Jack's voice exploded over the comm, booming across the bridge. "YES! I AM RIGHT! Why don't you two just go back to Miami!"

Breanna's disbelief erupted. She punched him three times, hard, on his bicep—each strike a fierce declaration of her fury. "What the hell is wrong with *you*? I told you, I didn't know Greg was here—we're not together. He lives a lifestyle that's... morally questionable. And I came back because I missed *you*, you jerk!"

A heavy silence fell, pregnant and suffocating, broken only by the steady hiss of the Orca's life support systems. Jack's face was unreadable, a mask concealing the storm beneath. Then, a single word slipped from his lips.

"Oh."

Chip cut through the tension, voice sharp and impatient. "What is happening right now? Maybe you could wrap this up later?"

The Rover CAM lens caught their sudden embarrassment as they turned away, scrambling to regain composure.

"Sorry," Jack muttered.

"Sorry," Breanna echoed, equally mortified.

Chip shook his head slowly, a weary smile tugging at the corners of his mouth. "Freaks."

Behind him, Greg stood silent, eyes fixed on the screen. The usual cocky assurance had fled, replaced by a shadow of deep disappointment.

Topside, tension hung thick like a storm about to break. Chip hunched over his iPad, a brooding oracle lost in flickering data, oblivious to Greg, Bobbi, and Sam pacing with restless agitation around him.

"What's goin' on down there?" Chip barked, his voice bouncing off the cramped steel walls of the Orca's deck.

"You got that right," Bobbi growled low, eyes sharp. "What kinda kinky stuff you into, Greg?"

Greg, ever the pragmatist, cut her off with a sharp, "Leave it alone, Bobbi."

Jack's voice crackled over the comms, crisp and

controlled: "Stand by."
Frustration boiling over, Chip released a guttural growl and flung his arms skyward, pure exasperation writ large.

Jack and Breanna rounded the corner, the reality hitting them like a physical blow—the narrow stairwell leading to the lower deck. "Watch out," Jack hissed, voice barely audible over the muffled gurgle of water. "Stay close. We could run out of space fast." The tight stairway felt like a descent into the unknown, claustrophobic and unforgiving. Rover, their bulky submersible, lurched forward with a sickening thud as it slammed into the doorframe. It reversed, then tried again—another jarring crash.
Chip's voice crackled urgently over the comms, panic rising. "Uh, Jack? Rover's… too fat."
Jack muttered, already switching to dive lights. The bottom loomed, blocked by another heavy metal door. He grabbed the handle and heaved with all his might. The door wouldn't budge. A second shove, more ferocious, his muscles screaming in protest. Nothing.
Breanna's hand touched his arm, light but urgent. Frustration carved deep lines into Jack's face as he turned. Her finger pointed to a detail he'd missed—a rust-eaten bolt lock clinging stubbornly to the top of the door. "Ugh!" The sound was a strangled groan of frustrated realization.
With practiced desperation, Jack pulled a small pry bar from his belt. The metallic crack-crack of

stressed metal came agonizingly slow. Finally, the bolt dropped free. The door groaned inward, a mournful sound echoing centuries of decay.

They slipped into darkness heavy with the stench of rot and the oppressive silence of the deep. The deck was a chaotic graveyard—splintered wood and broken furniture tossed aside as if by a furious, unseen hand.

"Huh," Jack breathed, voice tight.

Chip's frantic voice shattered the silence. "What? What? What's going on down there?"

"Crew's quarters," Breanna whispered, a shiver running through her despite the wetsuit. Disappointment weighed on them like a suffocating blanket.

"Let's keep moving," Jack said, voice barely audible above the water's gurgle. Their lights pierced the darkness like weak lances.

A bone-chilling dread settled over Breanna as they neared the bow. The silence, thick and suffocating, felt pregnant with something unseen. Her fins stirred the silt, sending a ghostly cloud swirling before settling to reveal a faint, almost imperceptible line snaking across the deck beneath layers of sediment. Her heart hammered.

Jack's face tightened with grim resolve. He pried open a hatch with a grunt. It swung inward with a groan that echoed hauntingly through the flooded hull, revealing a yawning abyss.

They exchanged a look of stark apprehension, the fear in their eyes unspoken. Descending into the inky blackness, the cold pressed in around them, a suffocating weight of the unknown.

The lower deck stretched out before them, an eerie expanse of emptiness. Broken barrels lay scattered against the hull, their rusted surfaces faintly gleaming in the beams of their dive lights. A gnawing frustration grew with each sweep of their flashlights, cutting through the silt-filled water in desperate, crisscrossing patterns. Then, Breanna's head snapped toward the far corner—a sudden, blinding flash of gold, a fleeting shimmer swallowed quickly by the gloom.
"Jack! Did you see that?" she whispered, her voice taut with disbelief.
"There!" Jack pointed, his hand trembling slightly. Breanna spun around, breath catching in her throat. Nestled deep in the shadows of the stern, partly hidden beneath decaying debris, lay stacks of broken crates overflowing with gold bars. Four massive chests, their surfaces encrusted with barnacles and sea growth, stood sentinel against the rear wall. The dive lights danced across the seabed, illuminating a breathtaking sight—the deck itself seemed dusted with golden particles, glimmering like a treasure lost to time.
As they drew closer, a sharp *whack* echoed through the confined space. Jack's hammer shattered the rust-eaten locks of the first two chests. The lids creaked open with heavy thuds, revealing dazzling hoards of gold bars and exquisitely crafted jewelry. Breanna gasped, words failing her.

Jack stared, his face frozen in stunned disbelief. The silence that followed was broken only by the pounding of their hearts—a fierce rhythm as relentless as the sea itself—bearing witness to the treasure they had uncovered, a secret guarded by the dark, silent depths.

Chip's voice crackled over the comm, breaking the reverent stillness. "Any time you want to throw us a bone? Come on, give me something!"

Breanna and Jack exchanged wide-eyed glances, exhilaration shining in their gaze. The gleam of gold reflecting off the submerged chests was almost blinding—enough to bring even the toughest man to tears.

"Send Sam to the armory. Get a couple of Glocks," Jack ordered.

"Guns? Guns? Why guns?!" Chip murmured, disbelief creeping into his voice.

Jack smiled, the weight of untold riches pressing down on him—a welcome burden. "I've got about... I don't know... a hundred million reasons. Maybe two."

Chip's eyes bulged in astonishment. The static crackle of the comms couldn't mask the raw excitement in his voice. "There's so much gold here, it's... it's biblical!"

Greg, Sam, and Bobbi gawked as Chip rolled onto his back, arms and legs flailing like a man possessed by a joyous, avaricious spirit.

"Yes! Yes! Yes!" he shouted, leaping to his feet, kicking, screaming, punching the air like a prizefighter who just won the heavyweight championship. Greg grabbed him before he could launch himself overboard.

"What the heck, bro?! Qué pasa?!"

Chip embraced Greg, showering him with a fervent kiss. Then, with the manic energy of a caffeinated hummingbird, he lunged at Sam and repeated the performance, before grabbing Bobbi in a bear hug and planting one on her too.

"Oh, no!" Bobbi gasped, more surprised than offended.

Chip shook Bobbi gently by the shoulders. "It's the mother lode, baby! The motherlode!"

He shook Greg with equal enthusiasm. "You morally questionable Sasquatch! We hit the jackpot!"

The deck erupted in chaos—high fives, whoops, and hollers echoed across the ocean, a wild celebration of the unimaginable fortune they had just discovered.

Seven miles west, aboard the sleek GO-FAST boat, Davis leaned casually against the wheel, a sinister grin spreading across his face. He set his high-powered scope carefully on the seat beside him, eyes locked on the distant vessel cutting through the water far ahead.

As shouts of triumph crackled through their comms, Breanna and Jack exchanged a glance, their smiles stretching as wide as the endless ocean around them.

"Is this real?" Breanna whispered, disbelief still lingering in her voice.

Jack snagged the iPad clipped to her dive belt. "Absolutely—for real." He grinned as he snapped a selfie of them standing beside the two overflowing chests, proof of their astonishing find.

Together, they filled two salvage bags with gold bars and glittering jewelry from the first chest. Greg expertly worked the crane while Chip carefully maneuvered the heavy bags onto the deck, his earlier wild excitement giving way to focused precision. Breanna assisted Jack and Sam with fresh air tanks, their practiced movements smooth and efficient after years of dives.

Once ready, Jack and Breanna slipped beneath the waves again, the cool water a welcome relief from the heat of their adrenaline-fueled success. They returned soon after with two more bags heavy with treasure from the second chest. Jack slid the empty chests aside, eyes sharp as he scanned every inch of the seabed, unwilling to miss a single secret hiding in the shadows.

Later, the tension hung thick in the air. Jack and Breanna moved methodically through the cramped space, each creak and groan of the aged ship echoing like a whisper of secrets long buried. Jack's flashlight sliced through the darkness, probing every shadowed corner, every hidden crevice. Breanna yanked open a closet door, only to be met with a swirl of silt and emptiness.

Then Jack's hand closed around a small, ornate wooden box tucked away beneath a loose floorboard. A flicker of hope sparked in their eyes as they set it gently on the floor. With careful fingers, Jack lifted the lid. Inside, only a few tattered shreds of what looked like ancient sackcloth remained. They exchanged a glance heavy with frustration, discovery had teased them, only to slip away at the last moment. The hunt was far from over.

Miles away, aboard the weathered Sea Wench, a covert operation was taking shape. Davis and four equally hardened crewmen formed a tight semicircle around Treese, their eyes cold and unyielding like sharpened steel.
"The bell," Treese growled, his voice a low, gravelly rumble. "We need it. Same drill as always. A hundred times before, and a hundred times we've pulled it off."
His face, etched with years of hard living, moved toward a heavy metal container, the others falling into step like shadows. "Stay dark," he rasped. "Get the goods. No collateral damage… at least not yet." With a quick snap, he opened the container, revealing a compact nest of C-4 blocks, wrapped with precise care and ready for use. "This time, I'm making an exception," he said, a sharp glint flashing in his eyes. "And LaPointe's on it."

The Past Is Not Buried

The late afternoon sun, molten gold in color, bathed the Orca's deck in a warm, glowing light. Breanna, her face reflecting the exhaustion of the day, expertly

maneuvered a pallet jack across the worn planks. Bobbi and Chip wrestled two overflowing salvage bags onto it, Chip cradling the gold like a newborn, careful not to drop a single bar.

Jack emerged from the dive platform, peeling off his gear, face flushed with the reflected glory of their discovery.

The crew gathered around, forming a stunned circle of awestruck men mesmerized by the glittering bounty laid out before them. Chip threw his arms skyward and let out a primal yell.

"YES!"

Their jubilant shouts echoed across the tranquil ocean, carried on the warm breeze.

"So, what are we looking at?" Chip asked, voice cracking with excitement as he rubbed his hands together like a hungry wolf.

"Ninety... maybe ninety-five million," Jack breathed, a grin splitting his face. "Insane..."

Chip was gob smacked, unable to find words.

"And that's only half of what's still on the galleon," Jack added, patting Chip on the shoulder, leaving him speechless. Suddenly, a jarring voice broke the revelry. "Jack, why the hell do we have guns on a research vessel?"

Jack snorted. "Smugglers? Pirates? You think you're gonna call 9-1-1 out here?" He leveled a hard look at

Chip, who swallowed hard.

"Point taken," Chip mumbled.

"Scarlett's tonight," Jack said, shifting the subject smoothly. "Bobbi and Sam are on security detail, provided we bring back enough boiled shrimp."

"Greg joining us?" Chip inquired.

Jack was quick to answer. "Negative." Message received loud and clear. Jack caught a faint whiff of something less than sea air and wrinkled his nose. "Chip," he said, "the co-eds might appreciate your enthusiasm, but when was the last time you showered?"

Chip looked bewildered, raised an arm, and sniffed. His face crumpled. "Sweet baby Ray..." He shuffled away, mortified. Just then, a video call popped up on a nearby monitor. The words "ALBATROSS CALLING" flashed across the screen. Will's face appeared, his expression grim.

"I've been trying to reach you," Will said, voice tight.

Jack sat down, a troubled look crossing his face. "What's wrong?"

Will's jaw tightened. "Breanna told me about Billy... I wish you'd told me, but I understand why you didn't. Captain's orders. But this... this rift between us... that's my fault."

Jack exhaled slowly, a weight lifting from his shoulders. But Will's words lingered, and a fresh worry etched itself on Jack's face. Do I tell Dad about the gold? His eyes flicked to the monitor's corner, where the sonar scan blinked silently, an unseen sentinel watching over them all.

The day had been a brutal marathon. Jack stepped

into the hot shower of his cramped quarters, eager to wash away the salt and grit of the Atlantic that still clung stubbornly to his skin—and even lingered on his lips. With a deep sigh, he pulled the smoked glass door closed behind him. Steam quickly filled the small space, swirling thick and warm. The water pounded against his body, slowly peeling away the exhaustion, the weight of the day beginning to lift. Then, a quiet click from the door handle cut through the steady rhythm of the shower. The slow creak of the door sliding open followed. Jack didn't need to turn to know who it was.

The door opened just a crack. In the dim hallway light, Breanna's eyes met his through the mist. She stepped inside with a calm familiarity, her presence steady and quietly reassuring. Her hand rested lightly on the edge of the shower door—no further intrusion, just there, a gentle anchor in the haze.

Jack glanced over at her, his features softening. "Everything okay?" His voice was low, almost a whisper.

She nodded, a faint smile teasing the corners of her lips. "Just checking on you."

"Washing away the weight of the day," he replied. Their eyes held in the humid silence, speaking volumes the words never could. The moment carried all the thoughts and feelings they'd been holding back, too afraid to voice aloud. Without another word, she stepped back quietly, the door clicking softly shut behind her.

Jack was left alone again, wrapped in the warm cascade of water and the fading echoes of the day.

Night At Scarlett's

Saturday night at Scarlett's was a maelstrom of sound and motion. The bar, a hundred years young yet pulsing with a primal energy as vibrant as the night it first opened in 1925, throbbed with life. Onstage, a girl with fiery red hair wielded an electric violin like a weapon, ripping into a ferocious rendition of The Who's *Baba O'Reilly*. The music was a pulsating heartbeat, coursing through the crowded room, electrifying every soul inside.

Chip burst through the tiki-shack entrance, Breanna and Jack close behind, their hands clasped tight. Their eyes darted around, assessing, scanning the vibrant chaos. Chip's gaze was sharp, predatory, slicing a path toward the bar. Breanna spotted Tom—a walking spectacle in a ridiculously loud tropical shirt, khaki shorts, and flip-flops—deep in conversation with Scarlett, the bar's owner. Scarlett was Southern charm incarnate, her long red hair flowing, her laugh rich and intoxicating like the rum punch she expertly poured.

Jack let out a low chuckle, swallowed by the roar of the music as they approached. Scarlett's smile widened, a beacon of welcome. Tom turned, eyes widening in surprise.

"You made it, Bubba! And look at you, Dr. Bonilla. Prettier than ever," he said, his voice barely audible over the din.

"Flattery will get you everywhere, Sheriff," Breanna replied, a playful glint sparking in her eyes.

Tom laughed, hearty and genuine. Breanna hugged

Scarlett, the embrace brief but intense.

"It's great to see you, Scarlett. I missed this place."

"We missed you too, sugar. Your usual?" Scarlett asked, eyes flicking toward Jack.

"You remember?" Breanna smirked.

"Are you kidding? Jack?" Scarlett laughed.

"Same," Jack confirmed, his voice tight with barely contained excitement.

"One beer and one margarita, coming right up," Scarlett said, the clinking of ice a sharp counterpoint to the relentless beat of the music.

As Scarlett mixed the drinks, Jack leaned close to Breanna, his voice dropping to a conspiratorial whisper. "Can I ask you a question?"

"Sure," Breanna replied, her heart beating a little faster.

"Do you buy into my dad's global warming theory?" he asked, a mischievous glint dancing in his eyes.

"Ooooo, mi Papi's putting on the moves," Breanna teased, her fingers tracing the line of his hand.

"The research is there," Breanna said, her voice suddenly serious. "Methane's a big factor."

Jack nodded, just as the music screeched to a halt. Randi, the bandleader—a whirlwind in ripped jeans, an AC/DC tank top, and long blonde hair—stepped up to the microphone. Her voice cut through the silence like a knife.

"We've got a good friend in the house, and I hear he plays a mean guitar," she announced, dripping with mischief. "How about we get him up here to crank one out with us?"

The crowd erupted in cheers.

Randi's gaze swept the room, landing on Jack at the bar. A pulse of anticipation rippled through the air.

"They want you, Jack!" Breanna whispered, barely audible over the rising applause.

Caught off guard, Jack glanced at Breanna. She gave him an encouraging nudge. A thrill, equal parts exhilarating and terrifying, shot through him.

"Go on, rock star," Breanna urged, eyes sparkling.

With a deep breath, Jack stepped through the cheering crowd onto the stage. His fingers trembled slightly as he picked up a guitar.

"What are we doing?" he whispered to Randi.

She grinned, a flash of teeth in the dim light. "Like I need to tell you."

The music exploded—a rip-roaring, heart-stopping version of Dave Matthews' *Ants Marching*.

Randi's violin screamed, Jack's guitar howled, and his voice soared above the music, raw and powerful.

The song ended in a crescendo of sound and applause. The crowd roared its approval.

Jack embraced Randi, then beaming, made a beeline for Breanna.

"That was awesome, babe. You killed it," she whispered, eyes shining with pride and something deeper.

He pulled her close, kissing her deeply, passionately. Taking her hand, he led her onto the crowded dance floor as the music shifted to Bob Marley's *Stir It Up*. Locking eyes, he drew her closer and lost himself in the rhythm, the moment, the electric energy of Scarlett's, the night pulsing all around them, full of music, mystery, and something dangerously close to forever.

Across town, down in the Orcas' galley—a cramped, claustrophobic space, even for two—an unspoken competition crackled between Sam and Bobbi. They sat on opposite sides of the scarred wooden table, their movements sharp, their eyes flickering like predators sizing each other up. Bobbi, a whirlwind of nervous energy, fanned her cards with a flourish.

"Go fish," she snapped, her voice tight.

Sam didn't look away. "I was thinking something nifty. Seventy-five feet."

"Go fish."

Bobbi's voice dropped to a low purr laced with steel. "Couple of bedrooms. Maybe a hot tub? Go fish."

"Yes, love, yes," Sam practically hissed, leaning forward, his hand hovering over his cards. "And a condo near Sydney Harbour."

Bobbi's smile vanished. "Sydney? No, no, no! I wanna live in L.A.! Be closer to my mama!"

Sam's jaw clenched, his face twisting into a grimace. The words burst out—harsh, sudden—"I'm not living in a smog pit!"

"Smog pit?!" Bobbi's voice cut through the room, sharp as shattered glass. "What are you talking about, boy?! I'll take SoCal over the bottom of the world any day! Any day!"

Sam slammed his hand down, scattering the cards. "Come on, Bobbi! I haven't even been home in five years! Work with me here!"

A heavy silence fell, thick and suffocating, broken only by the ship's rhythmic creak. The air between them crackled with resentments and desires left unspoken. Then Sam's voice dropped, a tentative lifeline thrown into the void.

"What about Hawaii?" he breathed.

Bobbi's eyes widened in surprise.

Then, unexpectedly, she burst into a relieved, almost hysterical laugh. Their smiles, when they finally came, were radiant but fragile, shadows of uncertainty lurking beneath.

A cold sweat slicked Bobbi's palms as she leaned back, the chair groaning under her sudden stillness. Sam narrowed his eyes, scanning his hand with meticulous care. The worn edges of the cards whispered secrets only he could read. Slowly, deliberately, he plucked a card from the deck. The snap echoed in the sudden quiet.

"Go fish," he said, the words hanging heavy, laced with chilling nonchalance.

Bobbi retreated to the counter in a frantic ballet—each step measured, each breath shallow. Sam took a long, slow gulp of beer, the amber liquid catching the dim light like a predator's eye. The drawer creaked open, but instead of silverware, twin Glock snouts gleamed menacingly in the shadows.

"What's wrong?" Sam's voice was deceptively calm, the question a barely concealed threat, hanging between them like a guillotine blade.

Suddenly, three figures—shadows clad in camouflage and ski masks—sprinted across the slick deck, their muted footsteps echoing against steel. Bobbi's breath hitched, a prickling unease lancing sharp and cold.

"Something's up," she whispered, her gaze sweeping the room. "We're the only ones here… aren't we?" She spun to Sam, her voice taut with tension. "I know this ship. We're not alone."

Sam slammed his cards on the table, a curse tearing through the silence. "Aw, hell."

With the practiced grace of a seasoned warrior, he

accepted the weapon Bobbi offered with a grim nod. The ease with which she checked the magazine and slipped the pistol into her waistband told a story— this wasn't her first rodeo.

"You check the gold," she hissed, eyes narrowed. "I'll hit the lab and meet you topside."

"No way," Sam growled, sliding a fresh clip into his own gun. "We stay together."

The galley door creaked open, spilling shadowed light into the narrow hallway beyond. They stepped inside cautiously, eyes adjusting to the dim. Without warning, a deck hatch at the far end burst open, flinging two figures into their path. Masked, tense, their eyes widened in surprise—then snapped shut with lethal intent.

Time fractured, slowed to a deadly crawl.

A deafening roar shattered the heavy silence, the sharp crack of gunfire ripping through the air.

Sam and Bobbi reacted instantly, diving for cover behind opposite doorways. The hallway exploded with a furious crossfire. Bullets screamed past, gouging the walls, sending chips of paint flying. The metallic tang of gunfire hung thick in the air, burning nostrils and tightening chests.

The camouflaged men, caught off guard, scrambled back toward the hatch, firing wildly. Their shots were desperate, reckless, and far less precise.

Bobbi's weapon barked back—one shot finding its mark with deadly accuracy.

Fueled by adrenaline and raw instinct, Bobbi charged down the hall, heart hammering.

"Bobbi, no!" Sam's desperate yell was swallowed by the chaos.

"This is not happening," he muttered, sprinting after her, every muscle coiled and ready.

On deck, chaos erupted into a storm of gunfire. The camouflaged men, frantic and desperate, swarmed the railing, leaping onto the dock in a frantic bid for escape. Against the cold moonlight shimmering on the water, Bobbi stood silhouetted, firing a final, relentless hail of bullets.

Then a searing pain tore through her shoulder. A scream ripped from her lips as she crumpled onto the deck.

A single, sharp shot echoed across the water.

"Bobbi!" Sam's voice cracked with panic. His own shots tore through the fleeing figures as they scrambled onto the dock, vanishing into the shadows.

He dropped to his knees beside her, horror etched deep into his face as he watched the dark bloom of blood spreading across her shoulder. Her pained gasps hung in the night like a death knell.

"Oh God..." he whispered, voice breaking.

The music swelled to a final, lingering chord, then faded into a silence thick with unspoken desires. Jack held Breanna close, his gaze locked on hers—dark and molten, charged with something raw and sensuous. "Why don't we finish those drinks and get out of here?" he murmured, his voice a low thrum against her ear.

Their return to the bar felt jarring, the energy shifting sharply. Jack's eyes flicked toward Chip, caught in a blur of tequila shots and giggling college girls clad in barely-there Florida State tank tops. Breanna's expression darkened, a storm gathering in her usually bright eyes. "Oh no," she whispered, the words fragile and raw.

The confession tumbled out—a torrent of fear and regret. "I made a horrible mistake. And I made it worse by running away. I was terrified of losing everything… afraid to tell Will… afraid of how you'd react… but mostly, I was terrified you hated me. And… a part of me died when I realized I'd lost the most important thing."

Jack's throat went suddenly dry. He stared down at the bar, watching the ice in his drink melt too slowly, as if time itself hesitated. Months of tension condensed into this moment. "I was angry," he finally admitted, his voice rough. "I thought we were done. How could I ever trust you again?" He looked up, meeting her gaze, and found her hand, holding it tight. "But now… I do trust you. And I never stopped loving you."

A slow, deliberate clap sliced through the silence. A long, ominous shadow fell across them.

"Well done, Jack. Well done. It's not Hemingway," a voice sneered, dripping with sarcasm.

They spun around to see Treese standing behind them, a predatory smirk twisting his lips. "Still, a captivating, tender moment. What I don't get, Doc, is why you want to be with this murderer?"

Jack exploded from his chair, fury blazing in his eyes. "That's it!"

"Jack, no!" Breanna cried, but it was too late.

Treese staggered back as Jack's fist connected with a sharp crack against his jaw. Blood blossomed on Treese's cheek, but he recovered quickly—a whirlwind of fists. Two brutal punches landed on Jack's face, sending him reeling, his nose bleeding.

Treese grinned cruelly, waiting for Jack to strike again.

Jack's eyes narrowed, cold fury replacing his earlier rage. He lunged—but Tom leapt between them, slamming Jack hard against the bar.

"Back off, son!" Tom roared, holding Jack in place. Then he faced Treese, voice low and dangerous. "What do you wanna do, Romer?"

Treese's smirk lingered briefly on Breanna, his gaze predatory, before he slipped away into the night.

Jack, seething, kicked over a bar stool in frustration.

A phone rang.

Breanna snatched it from her purse, face already pale. "Hello?"

Tom's voice cut through the chaos, a sharp warning. "Jack, listen to me. This isn't the first time he's tried to trap you. You can't fall for his merc intimidation tactics. He'll put a real good whooping' on you, boy."

Breanna held the phone to her ear, her ashen face saying more than words ever could.

Within moments, the trio scrambled back to the Orca, the ocean's roar a distant drum beneath the frantic pounding of their hearts. Breanna burst through the cabin door, Jack and Chip close behind her, their faces drawn and grim.

Bobbi lay slumped at the table, a stark white sheet drawn tight over her, stained with a spreading crimson blotch that screamed of how close she'd come. Sam knelt beside her, his jaw clenched, focused on the deep gash in her shoulder. Blood seeped through the flimsy fabric of her bikini top and shorts.

"My God, Bobbi, are you all right?"

Sam's voice was tight, edged with fear.

"She's damn lucky," Jack muttered, eyes locked on the wound. Bobbi winced, a strangled gasp escaping her lips. "Two inches over," she whispered, voice barely audible, "and you guys are splitting up my bank."

"Don't say that," Sam snapped, anxiety sharpening his tone. "What the hell, Sam?"

"Bobbi heard something," Sam explained, voice taut with strain. "We went to check it out, and then... a full-on gunfight broke loose."

"Did you see who they were?" Breanna demanded, sharp and urgent.

"No," Bobbi replied, voice clipped, her eyes burning with quiet fury. "Camo dudes, ski masks."

Jack's fists clenched. "I knew Treese was up to something." The unspoken threat hung thick between them.

Get The Goods

Chip stood pale and tense, eyes glued to the small sonar monitor. His knuckles whitened as he gripped the edge of the console. A low, guttural sound slipped from his throat. All eyes turned as he moved quickly to the larger screen, fingers flying over the keyboard. The sonar image shifted, then with a frantic flick, he activated the 3-D projector. The Galleon appeared, rotating slowly in midair. A sickening pit twisted in everyone's stomach as the image revealed nearly a quarter of the ancient ship teetering on the edge of a yawning ravine.

A collective gasp broke the silence, replaced by a stunned, horrified quiet.

"You've got to be kidding me," Breanna breathed, eyes wide in disbelief.

"That scan's from just before we left the site," Chip said, voice trembling. "I didn't have time to analyze it."

Breanna jabbed a finger at the screen. "There's methane venting right here. Jack, it could be a week, a day… or an hour. That ship's going into that ravine. We can't go back."

The weight of her words settled over them, thick and suffocating.

Jack's jaw tightened, determination hardening his features. "Bobbi, we need to get you to a hospital."

"And tell them what?" Bobbi's voice was sharp, defiant. "That I got shot guarding a pile of Spanish gold? No thanks."

Jack's eyes swept the group, steel flashing in their depths. "You're right," he said quietly, voice low and dangerous. "Sam, grab the shotguns."

"Jack, it's over! We have to get Sheriff Heller involved now!" Breanna pleaded, desperation rising.

"Sam and I will split guard duty. Two-hour shifts," Jack said, final. He didn't look at Breanna. Couldn't. Breanna grabbed his arm, pulling him into the hallway and slamming the door behind them. The silence inside the cabin was broken only by anxious whispers and exchanged glances among Sam, Bobbi, and Chip. The air crackled with unspoken fear.

Her grip on Jack's arm was a vise, knuckles white. Their whispers were swallowed by the oppressive stillness of the Orca's hull.

"If we go back down there," she whispered, voice barely audible, "we're dead. Dead, Jack. Even if we somehow survive the dive, Treese's goons will be waiting. They'll tear us apart." Her voice cracked. "I love you. But please, God, call Heller. Let him handle it."

Jack's eyes burned with anguish, desperate and fevered. He didn't hesitate—he lunged, pulling her into a crushing embrace. Relief flickered on Breanna's face—fragile and fleeting—cracking beneath the pressure of his intensity. She clung to him, eyes squeezed shut, a silent prayer escaping her lips. His kiss was fierce, demanding, leaving her breathless. His fingers dug into her shoulders as he whispered, choked with emotion:

"I love you. Everything. Everything depends on one more dive. Just one. We need that ship's name. Breanna, please. One last dive."

Her mind screamed—a chaotic battle of fear and love. She shook her head violently, trembling. The hug tightened, but her fingers clawed at his back.

Her whispered "Okay, Jack. Okay," was a broken promise—desperate, trying to calm the monster in his eyes. Yet in her gaze was a chilling contradiction—a silent scream of impending doom. The unspoken question hung heavy between them: Will they both survive this last dive… or will it be their last?

The stench of mildew clung to the cobblestones, mingling with something else—something metallic and sharp—that lingered in the cold night air as Greg made his way up the winding path. Hector's door stood wide open, a yawning black maw swallowing the faint, meager moonlight. A gut-wrenching dread sliced through him, cold and jagged, like shattered glass.
"Abuelo?" His voice cracked, a fragile whisper lost in the oppressive silence.
Inside, the living room was a war zone. Hector's oak easel, once a proud masterpiece, lay shattered on the floor, its vibrant moonrise painting now a grotesque parody—colors smeared, pigments crushed and bleeding into one another. The air hung heavy with the acrid tang of spilled oils, mixed with the sickly-sweet scent of ruined paint. Hector's cane, normally a steadfast companion, lay abandoned among the wreckage, like a fallen king's discarded scepter.
"Abuelo!" The scream tore from Greg's throat, raw and desperate, echoing hollowly in the ruin.
He stumbled into the dining room. It was worse there—an overturned table spilled its contents in wild chaos: trinkets and treasures, scattered and defiled, strewn like the remnants of a shattered life.

Greg's breath caught in his throat. Hector was gone. Vanished. And the silence that pressed down on him was suffocating—a weight too heavy to bear.

Dawn bled weakly through bruised, storm-ridden skies, casting a pale, sickly light over the deck. Jack stood on the bridge, bone-weary and haunted, the cold steel of his shotgun a thin shield against the rising tide of fear swelling inside him. Bobbi limped toward him, each step slow and heavy, her shoulder a crimson testament to the night's savagery. Her eyes—usually bright and fierce—were now dulled by exhaustion and a chilling premonition.

"You okay?" Jack's voice rasped, rough and raw.

"Sure," Bobbi said, tight-lipped, but the tremor in her voice betrayed her. "But—"

"It's 6:15. We give Greg ten minutes, then we're out." Jack's words were clipped, all business, but the slight shake in his hand told a different story.

"What about Breanna?" Bobbi's voice wavered, a desperate thread of hope woven through the question.

Jack's jaw clenched, the muscles twitching in slow tension. "What about her?" The words hung in the air, echoing the cold dread knotting his gut. "Sam said she bolted around four. Swore she'd be back. I've searched this damn ship. Even yelled at her on the cell. She's gone, Cap."

The silence between them grew heavy, suffocating. Jack turned away, his back stiff, trying to hide the icy grip of terror that tightened its claws around his chest.

A lone car sat in the empty lot before LaPointe Oceanic Research—a stark, accusing silhouette swallowed by the pre-dawn gloom.

Inside, the only light flickered from the monitor's eerie glow, casting ghostly shadows across Breanna's anxious pacing. Her face was a mask carved from sleepless hours, worry etched deep and sharp, haunted by a chilling premonition. Every glance at her watch, every nervous sweep of her gaze over the screen, was a silent scream echoing in the stillness. She clicked the mouse. The words *CALLING ALBATROSS* crawled across the monitor—a desperate plea swallowed by the vast digital ocean.

Will's arrival was quiet, almost unnoticed—a shadow slipping into the chair. His voice, usually easy and warm, was tight and strained now. His face was pale, like moonlight bleeding over fresh snow.

"You alone?" he asked softly.

Breanna nodded, the weight of unspoken guilt pressing down like a stone in her chest.

Will's tone hardened. "Breanna, you disappointed me. You're like a daughter to me. Jack loves you. I love you. But what you did... it crossed a line. You should have—"

"Will, Jack's in trouble!" Breanna snapped, panic sharp in her voice, cutting through his words like a blade.

Will went white.

Jack's boots thudded rhythmically against the deck, the shotgun a steady, ominous weight beneath his arm. Then came the sound—footsteps on the dock, heavy and deliberate, growing closer. Jack spun around, the shotgun rising instinctively.

"Whoa! Whoa! Whoa!"

Relief flickered across Jack's face as he recognized Greg, his grip easing but tension still taut like a drawn wire. Greg scrambled up the ramp, eyes wide with a terror deeper than fear.

"And just where have you been?" Jack's voice was rough, edged with suspicion.

Greg stepped onto the deck, taking in the scene—the shotgun, the charged air—with a look that crushed Jack's chest with its raw, soul-shattering fear.

"My Abuelo's place... it was trashed. And he's missing."

Jack stared, disbelief tightening around his throat. The shotgun suddenly felt heavier in his hands, the silence thick and suffocating, filled with a dread that swallowed them whole.

Breanna's anxious, pacing the room. She pulls out the bell she took from The Orca. Another bad decision? She places it in the one secure hiding place in the lab. Her face was a mask carved from sleepless hours, worry etched deep and sharp, haunted by a chilling premonition.

Breanna sat bathed in the cold glow of the monitor, her face a mask of hidden terror. She forced herself to speak, her voice barely more than a whisper.

"You have to leave now. Go to Sheriff Heller. Tell him everything. I'm on my way."

"And Breanna... please, be careful."

"Will... I'm so sorry." Her voice cracked with the weight of everything unsaid.

Will nodded grimly, eyes shadowed by a terrible understanding. Breanna clicked off the monitor, plunging the room into sudden darkness that made the tremor in her hand all the more pronounced. She drew a shaky breath, trying desperately to steady herself. Then she moved toward the door—

a rough hand clamped over her mouth, stifling her scream. Muffled cries spilled from her lips as two masked figures seized her, dragging her back into the shadows. The struggle was brief, a desperate flicker before the darkness swallowed her whole. Treese's heavy boots echoed down the hall, a cruel counterpoint to Breanna's terrified gasps. He stood there, eyes gleaming with a predator's hunger beneath a mask of feigned surprise. The tension in the air was so thick she could taste it—metallic, bitter, sharp against her tongue.

"A little bonus," he purred, his voice a velvet threat, fingers rough and calloused tracing a slow, deliberate burn along her cheek. The scent of his sharp, masculine cologne filled her nostrils—a sickeningly sweet prelude to violence.

"So, Doc," he sneered, voice low and growling like a beast ready to strike. "Fancy a swim with the sharks? A little... quality time south of the equator? Come now, commit. I know how much you adore the struggle."

Her scream—a raw, primal sound—was silenced by the sting of his slap. The sharp crack echoed off the walls, shattering the fragile calm before the storm.

"Tie her up," Treese ordered, his voice void of any mercy.

Breanna's screams were swallowed by the heavy thuds of masked men dragging her away, her desperate pleas fading into the growing darkness. Treese and Davis moved with ruthless precision— two predators in perfect sync.

Davis worked methodically, planting C-4 explosives with cold, clinical efficiency. Each placement was a death knell for the lab, a harsh percussion to the symphony of destruction. Meanwhile, Treese raged—a whirlwind of chaos. He overturned chairs, ripped open cabinets. The metallic screech of tearing metal and the sickening rustle of papers fluttering through the air filled the room. The stale scent of dust and old files stung Breanna's nostrils, even beneath the thick gag muffling her cries. He hurled damp wetsuits to the floor; their cold chill assaulted her senses from afar.

"Nothing here. The bell's on the Orca," Davis growled, voice edged with the icy certainty of a man who dances with death.

Treese's sharp gaze softened for a flicker, touched by something resembling curiosity. He knelt, eyes narrowing on a subtle discoloration in the carpet. A glint of steel—his knife—sliced through the oppressive stillness. With a savage rip, he tore open the floorboards, revealing a biometric safe. The cold steel gleamed in harsh contrast to the dusty floor. A predatory smirk twisted his lips as he pulled a block of C-4 from his pocket, the chilling weight heavy in his palm.

"Detonator," he barked, clipped and demanding. The pop of the detonator was tiny but swallowed by the deafening roar that followed. The safe's door exploded inward. Treese exhaled triumphantly. "Would you look at this," he breathed, drawing out the bell—the prize of their brutal hunt—his grin a predator's victory amid the smoky aftermath.

The engine of the black van thundered to life—a guttural beast awakening in the predawn gloom. Tires screamed against the cracked pavement, skidding with desperate fury.

The lab exploded into a fiery inferno, flames licking hungrily at the sky, smoke billowing upward like a dark, twisting pillar. It was a savage monument to their audacious heist—raw, merciless, and unstoppable. Their escape was a brutal victory, carved out in fire and chaos.

Call In The Cavalry

A tempest, raw and brutal, lashed at the Orca as she tore through the churning sea. Salt spray stung Jack's face like a thousand jagged needles as he clung to the bow, muscles trembling against the relentless assault. Inside the cramped bridge, Greg fought the wheel, his knuckles ghostly white, sweat mingling with rain as his every breath came sharp and ragged. Nearby, Bobbi's frantic fingers danced over the controls—a macabre ballet of desperate hope and trembling resolve.
On deck, Sam loomed like a shadow against the roaring storm, hoisting dive gear with slow, heavy movements. Each weight felt like a leaden anchor, mirroring the dread sinking deep in his chest. All of them wore the same haunted expression—the pale, haunted look of men staring straight into the face of death.

The marina was a maelstrom of wind and rain, a relentless deluge that blinded and chilled to the bone. Tom hunched against the onslaught, his yellow rain gear a flimsy shield against nature's fury. He clutched his phone like a lifeline, the screaming wind clashing with the urgent voice crackling through the speaker. With a frustrated slam, he shut the phone, the finality of the action echoing the sense of doom gathering thick in the air.
Two figures, shadows swallowed by the storm, leapt from the Albatross, their movements sharp and efficient as they hurried to secure the vessel. Will's face was a mask of grim anticipation as he strode

toward Tom. Their hurried words were swallowed whole by the gale, lost to the wrath of the tempest. "Breanna? Where is she? Why wasn't she with you?" Tom's breath caught in his throat. "Will... there was an explosion... at your lab."

The words, carried harshly on the wind, struck Will like a series of brutal blows. He froze, the color draining from his face—pale against the relentless gray of the storm.

"Her car... it was in the lot. The fire department... they're there now."

Grief, raw and visceral, tore at Will's chest. A silent scream trapped behind his eyes, which he desperately tried to shield. The rain poured down in an unyielding torrent, mirroring the tears he couldn't—and wouldn't—let fall.

"I have to get there."

Tom's grip tightened on Will's arm, a desperate plea. "Look, we don't know anything for sure. Let our people handle this. I've got a Coast Guard cutter ready, just like you asked. But where the hell are we going?"

Will swallowed the suffocating despair and managed a choked whisper. "She gave me the coordinates..."

They vanished into the storm, two figures running blindly through the deluge, rain baptizing them in misery. Tom fumbled with the truck keys, clumsy hands betraying his concern for Will, torn between hope and the chilling certainty of what awaited them. Will stood frozen—a statue of grief beneath the unforgiving sky—rain washing away his strength, his hope. The truck's engine roared to life, a defiant growl against the fury of nature, and they were gone.

Jack zipped up his wetsuit and walked toward the door of his quarters. Passing the bed, he noticed a light flashing on his cell phone. He picked it up. The screen read: TEXT — Tom.

Curious, Jack tapped the screen and read the message: *"Jack, there was an explosion. Your lab was destroyed. Breanna's car was there. Please get back and tell me she's with you."*

Jack's face drained of color. He staggered back onto the bed, pressing CALLBACK. The screen blinked: NO SERVICE.

Jack stared at the phone a moment longer before letting out a primal grunt, hurling it against the wall..

The Coast Guard Cutter shuddered beneath Will's feet, the metallic groan a low, steady thrum beneath the relentless crash of waves against the hull. Tom's face was carved with grim determination, though his voice carried a forced calm as he guided Will through the throng of crewmen. Whispered murmurs, tinged with awe and suspicion, slithered around Will like icy tendrils. Salt and diesel hung heavy in the air, sharp and biting, mingling with the unspoken tension. Celebrity? Far from it. Will felt only the crushing weight of lives hanging in the balance.

Captain Caldwell stood ramrod straight at the helm, his weathered face a roadmap of sun and storms. His eyes—stormy sea gray—pierced them with unsettling precision. The air between them crackled, thick with unsaid words.

Tom's handshake crushed bone. "Mike, how are you? This is Dr. Will LaPointe." The introduction felt brittle, like fine china trembling on the edge of shattering. Caldwell's gaze lingered on Will a moment too long before he gave a curt nod. "Doctor LaPointe. A pleasure… sir." The formality was strained, laced with skepticism that mirrored the silent judgment from the watching crew.

"Thanks for your help," Tom growled low. "Romer Treese. That name got our attention. We've got a dozen men, geared for war, standing by. Ready to rumble." The image of those grim-faced, heavily armed men flashed through Will's mind like a warning.

"Please understand," Tom added, his voice raw with a vulnerability that chilled Will to the bone, "five of my crew are on the Orca—including my son."

"Understood," Caldwell said, his voice tight with tension. "Tom, you've been on Treese's ship?" The question hung heavy with suspicion.

"Searched it a few days ago," Tom replied, jaw clenched. "Came up empty."

"Can you brief my men on the ship's blueprint?" Caldwell's tone bore the full weight of command—and the unspoken threat of failure.

"You got it." Tom's eyes pleaded, silently acknowledging the heavy burden he was placing on Will.

"Go. I'll be fine," Will whispered, voice fragile but resolute against the turmoil churning inside him. Tom and Caldwell slipped through the door, leaving Will alone in the eye of the storm. The bridge was a chaotic symphony of flashing lights and humming machinery, spinning around him. He felt exposed— just a lone scholar thrown into a brutal game of life and death.

He turned to the young seaman who had escorted

them, a boy whose wide eyes reflected a trembling mix of fear, fascination, and—something like hope.

"Private," Will's voice dropped low, steady, and commanding.

"Sir?" The youth's voice quivered.

"Would you mind showing me the dive room?" Will's gaze was sharp, unwavering. The dive room, the sea—they were his only hope now.

The rain wasn't just intensifying—it was exploding. A deluge unleashed. Wind howled like a screaming banshee, tearing at the deck. The Orca groaned and bucked beneath the assault. Sam's face was etched with grim determination as he threw open the dive gate. Instantly, icy spray stung his exposed skin. He scanned the churning void ahead, the empty deck a swirling canvas of gray, and waited. Waited for what felt like an eternity—salt spray stinging his eyes, fear's bitter taste clinging to his tongue.

Jack emerged from the hatch. The harsh light caught the glint of his knife and the ominous bulge of the salvage bag slung low on his hip. His face—usually lit with reckless humor—was drawn and gaunt, eyes burning with feverish intensity. The storm swallowed Sam's shout, a desperate cry swallowed by elemental chaos.

"Jack! Are you insane? I can't let you go down there!" A monstrous wave—a wall of green fury—crashed against the hull. Icy sea spray coated them both, brutal and unrelenting. Jack, dazed but unyielding, stared past Sam, his gaze fixed on some unseen horror. The red in his eyes wasn't just from salt spray—it was the fire of a man teetering on the edge of obsession.

"Hear me?! This is suicide!" Sam roared, voice cracking with a mix of fury and fear.

Jack's eyes snapped to Sam at last, the feverish haze replaced by a cold, calculating glint. "I need you up here. But if anyone tries to board... shoot them. Every. Last. One." The casual brutality of the threat sent a chill straight through Sam's bones. This wasn't the Jack he knew—this was a man driven by something far darker than greed.

Despite the icy dread clutching his heart, Sam helped strap the double tanks onto Jack's back, his hands trembling slightly as he fitted the helmet, the cold metal biting into his skin. He clipped the crane cable to Rover, the submersible, their mechanical lifeline into the churning abyss.

Chip, hunched over the control panel like a pale, nervous wreck, adjusted Rover's controls, knuckles white against the plastic. Jack's image flickered on the large monitor—ghostly, framed by snow-filled static.

"Can you hear me, Jack? Do you read?" Chip's voice was strained, laced with fear.

The crackle of the comms swallowed everything but the roar of wind and the pounding waves.

"While I appreciate the concept of independent wealth, I'm not at all enthusiastic about the prospect of..." Chip began, voice trembling.

The picture snapped clearly. Jack's face, illuminated by the rover's harsh light, was a mask of grim determination.

"Chip. Shut. Up." His voice was a low growl, laced with lethal quiet menace.

Chip's already pale face flushed a ghastly crimson. "Yep." He shrank back into his chair, a bead of sweat tracing down his temple. The weight of Jack's unspoken threat hung heavy in the air.

A monstrous wave— a liquid leviathan — crashed over the deck. Sam's face hardened into a mask of desperate calculation. Without hesitation, he hurled Rover, his loyal, battle-scarred German Shepherd, into the churning abyss. The rover vanished beneath the roiling waves — and then, as if some malevolent god had flipped a switch, the relentless drumming of rain abruptly ceased. An unnatural silence fell, heavy and suffocating.
Sam's gut twisted with a primal fear he barely understood as he stalked toward the bridge. He sniffed the air, catching the coppery tang of blood mingled with the sickly sweet stench of decay.
"What the hell is that?" His eyes fixed on the cobalt water swirling below, his breath caught. A few sluggish bubbles, like dying breaths, broke the surface.
The Rover, a dark phantom slicing through the thick, murky current, lit the way. Jack, lungs burning, muscles screaming, gripped the groaning crane cable with a death grip. He scanned the desolate underwater wasteland, and a cold dread clawed at his chest, paralyzing terror settling deep within. Nothing. No flicker of darting silver fish, no crustacean scuttling across the seabed. Nothing.
A vast, sickening emptiness. Methane, the silent killer, had transformed this vibrant ocean into a graveyard. Static crackled and spat in his comm unit, a desperate, dying gasp of technology.
Through a ghostly teal haze, the skeletal remains of the Galleon loomed, a macabre monument to

forgotten tragedy.

Jack reached the main deck, the bridge rising before him like a shadowed monolith.

The small rover, a spectral guardian, hovered beside the bridge as Jack examined the ship's wheel. His fingers traced the cold, barnacle-encrusted metal, searching for answers etched in rust and decay. He swung his dive light in slow arcs, the beam slicing through the inky blackness, revealing a deck strewn with death's debris. The front wall, once proud, now bore the silent scars of some unimaginable horror. A profound, gut-wrenching loneliness settled over him — a stark testament to utter desolation.

"I'm going below," Jack rasped, his words swallowed by the crushing pressure of the abyss. His voice — a hollow echo in his ears — fought against the ocean's relentless roar.

A razor-thin beam sliced through the inky blackness of the portal, revealing a cavernous treasure room. The chill of the swirling water wrapped around him like an icy shroud. He propelled himself forward, his dive light carving frantic circles across decaying chests — skeletal sentinels frozen in time.

The ancient timbers of the galleon screamed — a brutal symphony of grinding metal and splintering wood, a sound clawing at his sanity, scraping deep against his soul. He fought to stay afloat, his heart pounding a frantic drum in his chest, eyes darting wildly through the suffocating darkness for any sign of impending doom. The silence that followed was worse — a pregnant pause, thick with dread, before the next violent blow.

He reached the chests, breath hitching. One lay

empty and gaping, revealing a loose backboard. His gloved fingers, numb with cold, pried it free. Centuries-old silt dusted his hand as he scrubbed the blackened wood, uncovering a brand seared deep into the timber — *ARABELLE*. The name, ancient and cursed, pulsed with dark energy.
"She is the Arabelle!" The truth hit him like a thunderclap.
"Chip! Do you copy? Chip, come on, man!" His voice cracked — a desperate plea swallowed by the unforgiving depths.
Silence. Suffocating, deafening silence pressed down like a physical weight. His lungs burned. He was drowning in the quiet.

The sonar monitor pulsed with malevolent red: a horrifying real-time portrait of the ravaged galleon, half its hull teetering precariously over a yawning ravine. Chip's headset lay abandoned, Rover's controls untouched on the console — grim relics of a sudden, violent end.
The terrible finality of a death knell echoed through the chaos.
Through the swirling vortex of water and terror, the Sea Wench closed in. Sam, Bobbi, and Greg — silhouettes against the fury of battle — traded shots with desperate, furious grace. Thirty yards... twenty... the gap closing fast.
A torrent of brass-jacketed death, a hurricane of lead ripped from the bellies of Treese's men, their AK-47s spitting incandescent fury. The acrid smell of cordite burned the air, stinging Greg's nostrils, mixing with salt spray and the coppery tang of fear.
Greg, Sam, Bobbi, and Chip — knuckles white as

bone — flattened themselves against the deck. Bobbi's scream wasn't just sound; it was a raw, primal shriek clawing at the sanity of everyone within earshot, swallowed by the cacophony of gunfire.

"Stay down! For God's sake, stay down!" Sam snarled, voice tight with controlled rage masking crippling terror.

Then the sudden silence — deafening, suffocating — broken only by the frantic thumping of their hearts. Chip and Bobbi exchanged a look — a silent communion of horror etched into wide, desperate eyes.

A voice. Not just a voice — Treese's, amplified by a monstrous bullhorn, reverberating through their bodies like a physical blow. It shook the very soul from them.

"Orca! Prepare to be boarded!"

Sam's grim face scanned the deck. "Anyone hit?" His voice was a guttural growl, barely audible above the pounding sea. They stared back, mouths agape, eyes wide with terror so profound it stole their breath.

Fear hung in the air — alive, suffocating.

Treese's voice boomed again, slicing through the chaos like shards of ice.

"Surrender the Orca, LaPointe — and I won't kill the old man!"

The threat hung thick in the air, suffocating and sharp.

"Oh, God, no!" Greg's voice cracked, raw panic spilling out as he exploded upward—
a human missile fueled by blind desperation.

The Sea Wench loomed just yards away, a black shadow riding the savage waves.

At its bow, Davis stood steady, weapon cold and
ruthless— a pistol pressed against the frail form of
an old man—Hector, Greg's grandfather—
pale, drawn, his life seeping away with every
agonizing second.
Greg's scream tore through the storm—
guttural, desperate, a cry ripped from the core of
love and despair.
"Abuelo!"
The world tilted. The gun. The haunted eyes of the
old man.
The creeping darkness closing in.
They were utterly, irrevocably, horrifically doomed.
A guttural grunt tore from Jack's throat as he hoisted
the salvage bag—
a mountain of gold bars groaning with the weight of
their greed—onto his shoulder.
The splintered Arabelle board jabbed cruelly into his
neck.

The ship shrieked a monstrous, grinding groan
vibrating through his bones— a symphony of
tortured wood and looming doom.
Cold, clammy fear slicked his skin.
Jack staggered, vision blurring under the weight of
exertion and water.
He kicked out—a brutal, desperate shove—
the heavy bag dragging him across the slick deck,
every step a battle against the tilting ship.
With one last surge, adrenaline driving him forward,
he lunged through the portal—
a gaping maw ripped open in the ravaged hull—and
plunged into suffocating darkness.
The living quarters were a flooded tomb.

Icy water bit into his skin, the stench of decay and salt choking the air.

Each stroke was agony.

He hauled himself up the groaning stairwell, muscles screaming, vision narrowing.

Then he saw Rover—hulking and inert—guarding the gun deck entrance like a rusted sentinel.

"Come on, come on, where are you?" His voice cracked, a ragged gasp born of desperation and simmering fury, clawing back against the paralyzing fear.

He slammed the crane cable onto Rover's winch.

The heavy *thud* echoed in the deathly silence.

Weight dragged Rover down, jamming it hard into the doorway.

The ship shuddered violently—a spasm of dying agony threatening to tear it apart.

Jack froze, panic tightening like an icy fist around his heart, a wild prayer fighting the rising tide of despair.

The gold. The Arabelle. The risk... all suddenly meaningless against this brutal, unforgiving end.

The Sea Wench groaned against the Orca's steel flank.

Salt spray, sharp as needles, lashed both vessels.

Chip, Sam, Bobbi—faces etched with terror—and stoic Greg, wrists bound tight with cruel, biting cable, watched, paralyzed, as Treese emerged from the storm-wracked waves—a shark in a black wetsuit.

He moved with predatory grace, cold and merciless light gleaming in his eyes.

"Where's LaPointe?" Treese's voice rasped, slicing

through the wind's howl.
Silence.
Then— the sickening crack of bone.
Treese's rifle butt connected with Sam's skull in a brutal percussion that echoed over the pounding rain.
Sam crumpled, breath escaping in a ragged gasp, eyes rolling back into shadow.

Below deck, Jack's muscles screamed as he heaved against the solid oak doorway—Rover, an unyielding barrier blocking his path.
His powerful fingers dug into the slick steps, clutching for purchase.
A primal roar tore from his chest, raw and desperate, as he strained every ounce of his strength.
Then—the sharp *snap* of the bag's clip breaking loose, a small sound swallowed instantly by the thunderous *CRASH* of gold bars exploding from their confines.
The impact slammed into him like a freight train, knocking the breath from his lungs and sending him sprawling down the stairs.
The crushing weight of a king's ransom pressed down, dragging him into an abyss of darkness and agony.
His dive light—a flickering, fragile spark against the overwhelming blackness—faltered... then died.
On the Sea Wench, a cabin door groaned open, spilling shadow and menace.
Treese stepped through, his eyes ablaze with a cold, predatory hunger that sent a shiver straight to Breanna's core.

The rough rope bit cruelly into her wrists, the gag choking her voice—
but nothing compared to the icy dread tightening like a vise around her chest.
He advanced with slow, deliberate steps, his gaze lingering on her like a hunter marking prey—possessive, brutal, a ruthless lust that made her heart slam against her ribs, a frantic bird trapped in a cage of terror.

Last Chance

"Wetsuit. Now," Treese snarled, the words snapping like a whip against Breanna's simmering fury.

His eyes—cold, hard chips of flint—raked over her, the sharp tang of salt and ozone thick in the air.

No time for hesitation.

Breanna's disgust radiated like a physical force as she yanked the neoprene from the closet.

The coarse material scraped against her skin, a cruel betrayal.

Treese's thumb idly traced the serrated edge of his knife, sending a shiver spiraling down her spine.

On deck, Hector—like a broken marionette—was hauled by Davis, his blackened eye a brutal signature of Treese's cruelty.

Greg's ragged gasp cut through the rising wind, stabbing Breanna's gut.

"Abuelo... what did they do?"

The ocean roared its savage assent as Treese and Breanna, sleek predators in diving gear, plunged into the churning gray.

Davis's gaze flickered briefly to the Sea Wench, a terrifying mix of calculation and dread etched on his face.

"Sandoval! Gold. Now. Take Papi with you. And the C-4."

His voice was a low, guttural growl that echoed through the storm's fury.

"The Orca's going down, mate. Too bad."

The earth rumbled beneath them, louder than the storm—an ominous groan of something far worse to come.

Davis's pale face under the relentless rain betrayed the grim truth: the sea held secrets far darker than Treese's merciless cruelty.

A single, malevolent beam cut through the roiling water.

Breanna, a phantom of rage, led the way—her movements fluid and lethal, like a viper's strike.

They reached the mid-deck's gaping maw—darkness swallowing all hope.

"Down here," she hissed, voice tight with barely contained wrath.

Treese's grip on her arm, brutal and swift, was a cold reminder of her chains.

Her scream was swallowed by the depths as the cable tie snapped tight around her wrists, binding her to the railing.

"Insurance," Treese growled, voice void of mercy, as he slipped into the abyssal black.

Below, darkness reigned. Jack LaPointe lay sprawled among the scattered gold bars, his dive light flickering like a dying ember in the black abyss. Suddenly, his eyes snapped open—wide, filled with a terror that mirrored the storm raging far above. The dive light steadied, casting a narrow beam through the shadows. Two sharp taps echoed—a silent defiance against the crushing silence.

"LaPointe," Treese's voice boomed over the comms, calm and cold as a predator stalking its prey. "Ever wondered what it's like to die at the bottom of the ocean?"

Another, more violent rumble tore through the silence. The wreck shuddered beneath him—a bone-jarring groan that echoed with the promise of cataclysm. Jack's blood ran cold. He'd heard that sound before. He knew exactly what it meant. The ocean was coming for him. His life, his soul—all destined to sink into the unforgiving depths.

Through the suffocating fog, the Coast Guard Cutter *Zephyr* emerged, its massive form vibrating the very air with approaching menace.
Then came Caldwell's voice—not just a boom, but a raw, guttural bellow, amplified through the bullhorn like a physical assault, tearing through the silence and mist.
"This is the United States Coast Guard Cutter *Zephyr*!" The words hung heavy in the damp air.
His voice roared again, a final, shattering decree.
"This is your last chance. Surrender—or face the consequences. I will personally see to it that you feel every single one." The threat wasn't empty—it was carved into the grim lines of his face, forged in the cold steel of his gaze. The *Zephyr*, a monstrous guardian, loomed closer, its power absolute.

Davis and his four camo-clad psychos burst onto the deck—a whirlwind of adrenaline and assault rifle steel. AK-47s snarled, a symphony of impending death. The acrid bite of cordite filled the air, mixing with the stench of salt and fear. "Let's take 'em out!" Davis roared, his voice a guttural growl. A shared glance, a curt nod—the unspoken pact sealed in the cold light of imminent carnage. They squeezed off their first bursts—a dozen soldiers, faces twisted in terror, erupted from the cutter's belly, a wall of lead returning fire. The metallic shriek of bullets tore through the storm.

"Not today," Davis breathed, the bitter taste of defeat already on his tongue.

From the bridge window, Tom and Will watched the chaos—a macabre ballet of death. Will's binoculars, cold metal against his skin, scanned the *Orca*'s bridge. "I don't see Jack." Panic clawed at his throat. "Maybe he's below." He slammed the binoculars down, the sharp click echoing his frantic heartbeat, and bolted.

"Will, no!" The rising inferno swallowed Tom's shout.

The ship shuddered, a monstrous groan of twisting metal. Treese, clinging to *Rover*, felt the earth—or rather, the sea—shift beneath him. A deafening rumble, then silence—heavy, pregnant with dread. He wrestled *Rover* free and plunged into the claustrophobic stairwell; the darkness was a living, suffocating entity. His dive light sliced through the inky black, illuminating scattered gold bars glittering like cursed treasure in the gloom.

Treese propelled himself through the water, his light a frantic searchlight in the abyss. The ship groaned again, a death rattle. He reached the treasure room, a gaping maw of impenetrable shadows, kicked in, and disappeared headfirst into the suffocating dark. Only the faintest glimmer of Treese's dive light pierced the blackness. Deathly stillness reigned, broken only by drifting silt swirling like ghostly apparitions in his wake. Then, from a shadowed corner—light. Jack, red-faced and gasping, clawed his way out from under a pile of rubble. A torrent of CO_2 bubbles burst upward, a frantic testament to his terror.

He scrambled, dive light sputtering, groping blindly through debris—planks, sand, gold—in a desperate search for that crucial board. He glanced back: a searing beam sliced toward him from the portal—his escape closing fast. Despair etched itself on his face. He kicked toward the stairs, a desperate burst of energy, shooting up the passage with the darkness closing in behind him.

He reached the gun deck. *Rover* lay on its side, crane cable still attached, motor silent, light shattered. A beam snaked toward him from below. Jack spun, kicking furiously, pumping through the suffocating dark, past looming cannons toward the main deck hole. The ship rumbled again—a sickening grind threatening to tear it apart. He snatched up a cannonball, a single piece of solid metal in this maelstrom of chaos, as others rolled past.

He launched himself toward the deck hole, clutching a splintered plank, eyes wide with horror.

"No, no, no. Breanna!" He pushed out. Treese erupted from the hole below, propelled by desperate energy.

"Jack, look out!" Breanna screamed.

Treese grabbed Jack's dive tanks; the two men locked in a desperate underwater struggle, their fate hanging precariously in the balance.

Treese contorted, launching a savage kick like a projectile. Rotten wood groaned under the impact as he pivoted, slamming a brutal hammer fist into Jack's gut—a sickening thud echoing in the confined space. Jack retaliated; the cannonball whistled past Treese's masked face, a glancing blow that sent a jolt of pain through him. Ignoring the sting, metallic blood on his tongue, Jack ripped the knife from his dive belt—a silver streak in the dim light. He charged, a blur of motion, slicing across Treese's arm. A ragged groan tore from Treese's throat—raw, animalistic; a crimson blossom bloomed on his skin. Jack swung again. Treese's grip was a vise, seizing Jack's forearm and slamming it into the splintered deck with bone-jarring force. Jack screamed—a primal shriek ripped from his lungs—the knife clattered away as his hand impaled itself on jagged wood—a white-hot brand of pain. Treese pinned him, crushing weight pressing him against damp planks. Jack's eyes wild with agony, he clawed blindly for Treese's air hose, desperate—a guttural plea choked off by Treese's knee, driven with brutal precision into his groin.

A wave of nausea washed over Jack; his face twisted into a mask of pain. Breath stolen, vision blurring. "For Malcolm!" Treese growled, a guttural rasp dripping with venom. "My brother's dead, and it's time you pay!" Two more knees, targeted with savage efficiency, found their marks. Intense agony rendered Jack speechless, his body wracked with spasms. Air burned in his lungs—a silent scream trapped in shattered flesh. Treese's taunts became a cruel symphony. "Not enough, Jack! Did you think I'd let Malcolm go?!"

Breanna's voice cut through the chaos, desperate: "Stop! It was me!"

Treese's head snapped toward her, surprise flickering in his eyes, replaced instantly by cold calculation.

"Doesn't really matter now."

He released Jack—the sudden absence of weight a slight relief.

Breanna thrashed, terror palpable, eyes wide with desperate fear mirroring Jack's agony. As Treese moved, predator's grace in motion, her fear deepened into paralyzing dread.

"Revenge can be bittersweet," Treese murmured, voice low and dangerous. He grabbed Breanna's hair, yanking her head back until her eyes met Jack's. "But karma? All you have to do is wait for it."

With a sickening rip, Treese tore the mask from Breanna's face, revealing raw terror etched on her features. A guttural sob escaped her lips, followed by a furious curse.

She fought the cable ties binding her wrists—desperate, blood welling around raw chafed wounds. The discarded mask hung behind her head—a grim reminder of the fate closing in.

The timbers shrieked—a grotesque grinding of wood against unforgiving rock, a sound that tore at the soul. Treese forced himself back onto Jack, his weight a cruel lever pressing down on Jack's impaled hand. A guttural scream ripped from Jack's throat, primal and raw, swallowed by the groaning wreck all around them. The ship heaved, tilting sickeningly, threatening to spill them into the abyss below.

Treese, a predator amid chaos, ripped a brutal-looking tool from his belt—a wickedly pointed hammer, its head a blunt, obscene parody of mercy. He twisted Jack's helmet, forcing the shattered gaze of his victim to meet Breanna's.

"See the symmetry, Jack?" Treese snarled, his voice a venomous whisper over the rising cacophony of the collapsing ship.

Blood bloomed in the churning water; Jack gasped, a desperate, rattling sound, his legs thrashing weakly. Breanna, her strength failing, coughed—white bubbles of exhaled CO_2 rising like ghostly sighs. Treese brought the hammer down. Crack! The splintering wood shattered, swallowed by the escalating roar of the ship's death rattle. The groaning intensified—a symphony of destruction as the galleon pitched violently toward the stern. Treese leaned in.

"Ever read *Moby Dick*, Jack? 'That one most perilous and long journey ended.'"

He raised the hammer, its metallic glint a harbinger of doom.

Then—a whirring sound, a thwack. A harpoon exploded through Treese's hand, taking two fingers with it. A roar of agony tore from him, desperate and guttural. The hammer, severed flesh, and blood drifted away, fountains of crimson staining the water.

Will appeared at the bulkhead, eyes blazing with crazed fury, harpoon gun clenched in his grip—a whirlwind of pure, unadulterated vengeance. Treese screamed—a counterpoint to the dying cries of the ship—as Will charged, a human battering ram, smashing him against the splintering deck. Fists collided in a brutal ballet of violence.

Jack's face was a mask of grim determination as he wrenched his hand free. The pain was immense—searing, white-hot agony—but it fueled his desperate fight for survival. He snatched his knife, the glint of steel flashing in the turbulent water, and raced to Breanna, clamping the mask over her face.

She exhaled, a geyser of CO_2 rushing from the mask, a desperate gasp of life replacing the silent struggle for breath. He slashed through the cable ties binding her.

"Dad, she's going over!" Jack's voice was raw, panic threading through it.

Treese and Will, locked in a deadly grapple, tumbled toward the gaping maw of the deck hole.

"Jack, get away!" came the frantic warning.

But Jack didn't hesitate. He charged into the maelstrom, a desperate act of defiance.

Treese, with the cold efficiency of a butcher, whipped a knife from his dive belt, plunging it deep into Will's stomach. A choked gasp escaped Will; his eyes bulged, shock and horror mirrored in their depths. Jack's voice cracked, a tortured mixture of anguish and fury.

"DAD!"

The galleon's bow reared—then WHOOSH—a maelstrom of churning water ripped Will and Treese from their feet, dragging them screaming into the abyss.

"DAD!" Jack's cry was swallowed by the chaos.

The galleon shuddered—a death rattle that echoed the agony in his soul. He fought the sucking vortex, fingers clamping onto Breanna's arm, a lifeline in the churning green hell. The ancient timbers groaned— a final, tortured sigh—before the ship—their ship— plunged over the precipice, a monstrous tombstone sliding into the jagged maw of the ravine below.

Jack and Breanna fought for breath, the icy grip of the current releasing them only to leave them spinning, adrift in a sea of grief. The shattered image of their discovery loomed as a stark silhouette against the dark ocean depths. On the surface, the rain had ceased, leaving behind a chilling stillness after the night's onslaught of gunfire.

Five figures—grim, implacable soldiers—herded Davis and his men onto the cutter. Chip, Greg, Hector, Sam, and Bobbi, faces etched with fear and grim determination, watched from the deck. The sudden, earsplitting whine of the crane's cable reel sliced through the silence. Heads snapped up.
"Move!" Greg's roar was raw and urgent.
The reel spun, a metal frenzy building to a crescendo of deafening sound before the sickening BAM! as it jammed. The Orca shuddered with a bone-jarring groan. Two bolts expelled with explosive violence tore through the air. Greg threw himself to the deck, the metallic tang of fear coating his tongue.
"Look out!" Bobbi's scream cut through the tense air like a knife.
They ducked—a desperate ballet of survival—as the crane, a metal behemoth gone rogue, groaned under impossible strain. Bobbi and Sam exchanged a desperate glance. The final bolts detonated. Freed from its moorings, the crane tore across the deck, a monstrous pendulum smashing through the stern bulkhead with a cataclysmic crash before plunging into the ocean with a sickening thud.

The churning water, a maelstrom of icy salt and silt, clawed at Jack and Breanna as they fought toward the cliff, the gruesome track etched into the rock a macabre guide. Jack's eyes burned with grief so raw it felt physical. They darted to the taut crane cable—a lifeline, a death sentence; he couldn't tell.

He reached the ravine's edge.

Then Treese erupted from the depths. Breanna's scream—a raw, animal sound—tore through the air as Treese, a whirlwind of rage and fury, slammed Jack against the unforgiving sea floor. The impact vibrated through Jack's bones, a crushing weight stealing his breath.

Breanna launched herself onto Treese's back, fingers like claws tearing at his oxygen line. He threw her off with brutal efficiency, his bloody hand a whirling fist connecting with Breanna's temple with a sickening thud—bone on bone. She crumpled, lifeless beside Jack.

Treese, a predator savoring his kill, lunged for the groggy Jack. His voice, a guttural rasp, cut through the chaos.

"It's on now, boy."

A figure—Will—his face contorted in agony, his stomach blossoming crimson, suddenly propelled himself from the ravine with everything left in him. Treese's sneer twisted into a chilling grin.

"But two fingers will be a small price to finally be rid of you all."

Treese snatched for Jack's air hose. Then Will, a whirlwind of unexpected fury and adrenaline, collided with Treese. Treese roared, spinning free— only to be seized and hurled toward the ravine's maw. Will's desperate struggle was punctuated by Breanna's eyes snapping open, her gaze locking onto Jack as he started to rise.

"Dad!" Jack's voice was a choked whisper, a prayer lost in the deep.

The crane—a monstrous metallic arm—hurtled past them, its boom a scythe of death smashing into

Treese and Will. The sickening crack of snapping necks echoed across the water, followed by the thunderous crash of the crane's base. Breanna's scream was swallowed by the churning depths as Treese and Will vanished beneath the ravine and the steel beast.

Jack and Breanna bobbed amidst the tide, staring into the abyss. Horror etched their faces, mirroring the blood blooming in the water. Jack, body screaming in pain, collapsed to his knees at the ravine's edge, the weight of loss crushing him beyond bearing. His grief—a suffocating shroud— promised a darkness far deeper than the churning ocean.

Salt stung Breanna's eyes, mingling with bitter tears streaming down her face. The crushing weight of silence pressed down—a physical force amplified by the frantic crackle of static tearing through Jack's comms—a digital scream mirroring the agony in her heart.

Chip's voice, strained and desperate, clawed through the static: "Jack! Do you copy? Dammit, Jack, talk to me!"

Jack remained unresponsive—a broken statue carved from despair. The ocean's roar amplified the rhythmic thump of his pulse in Breanna's ears. She felt the tremor in his injured shoulder beneath her hand, the bone-deep chill seeping into her flesh. Then she saw it—a glint of gold, half-buried in the grey sand—a cruel mockery of treasure amid their harrowing ordeal. A vision from his nightmare, the cruel truth materializing from the sea's cold embrace. A choked sob escaped him.

Chip's voice sliced through again, edged with panic:

"Jack—c'mon, man—we need you!"

Those words—harsh and urgent—jolted Jack from numb paralysis. With a groan, he dragged his one good hand through the sand, revealing more of the shimmering object. It wasn't just gold—it was a cross, heavy with ancient craftsmanship, each emerald a screaming shard of light against the gloom.

He stared at it—not seeing the precious stones but the ghost of lost hope, a bitter realization etched on his face. He offered the heavy cross to Breanna, the gesture utterly devoid of meaning.

A wave of nausea washed over Breanna as she took the cross, its icy weight a physical manifestation of Jack's sorrow. Then the frantic thrum of approaching divers cut through the underwater world—twin shadows in the blurry green—their bubbles a frantic counterpoint to the stillness of her grief.

A Legacy Restored

The sun finally pierced the grey clouds. The harsh reality of the dive platform—the rough hands of the Coast Guard, the sharp sting of antiseptic—hit Breanna in a brutal cascade. She clung to Jack's hand, feeling the tremor in his battered body, a physical echo of their shared trauma.

"Infirmary, now," the medic barked, voice devoid of sympathy. But Jack shook his head, rasping, "Just wrap it. I need to talk to my crew."

Tom stormed onto the deck of the Orca, his face set with grim determination, clutching a battered wooden box. The sight of Jack and Breanna froze him; his pale face drained further. The silent glance they exchanged spoke volumes — a shared understanding of immeasurable loss, tinged with agonizing relief.

The medics' ministrations blurred around them. Then raw, guttural emotion tore through the deck as Jack, drawing strength from somewhere deep, rose slowly. Head bowed, he embraced Tom.

"Dad saved me, Tommy," he choked, voice thick with feeling. "He saved us."

Tears finally broke free, streaming down Tom's weathered face. "Thank God you're both all right," he whispered, his voice tight with grief and relief.

Overwhelmed, Jack pulled Breanna close, his arms crushing her. "I love you," he murmured, voice raw. Repeating it again — a desperate plea against the tide of his trauma.

"Tom's message," Jack began, voice catching.

Breanna silenced him with a gentle finger to his lips,

holding him close. Her tears were a silent testament to their ordeal, the terrible price paid, and the fragile hope still flickering between them.

Chip burst from the hatch, a whirlwind of frantic energy, boots pounding the steel deck. He barreled toward Jack, the salty tang of ocean air thick in his lungs.

"Jack, you scared the—" His words caught in his throat. The faces before him were etched with sorrow that chilled him to the bone.

"What?" he rasped, a choked whisper lost in the suffocating silence.

Bobbi, Sam, Greg, and Hector converged, their initial relief shattering like fragile glass as their eyes locked on Jack and Breanna. Bobbi's face crumpled; silent sobs hit like physical blows. Tears welled, blurring the hard lines of her usual stoicism. The air crackled with unspoken dread, a weight pressing down on them all. Breanna, her face slick with tears, squeezed Jack's hand — a desperate lifeline amid the grief.

Jack's gaze dropped to the worn wooden box. Greg followed it, hands trembling as he opened the latch. The tarnished bell inside was cool beneath his touch. The inscription — "Arabelle" — leapt out, stark and undeniable. A collective gasp caught in the throats of Chip, Sam, and Bobbi.

Hector's ancient face, carved by time and sorrow, traced a finger across the bell's aged surface. A single tear slid down his deeply lined cheek.

"Our family," Hector's voice was low, gravelly, weighted with centuries, "has waited over three hundred years for this day."

Greg's voice, usually sharp and pragmatic, softened

with doubt. "Abuelo, we still have no concrete proof the wreck is the Arabelle."

Jack glanced at Breanna, her eyes mirroring his turmoil. With trembling fingers, she detached a gold cross from her dive belt — cold and heavy in Greg's palm. Hector took it reverently, tracing the intricate design. His lips moved silently as he read the inscription. His breath caught. Tears streamed anew.

"Abuelo, what is it?" Greg pressed, voice tight with apprehension.

Hector's voice cracked, barely a whisper:

"'To my blessed nephew Carlos. Safe journeys on the Arabelle. Your loving uncle, King Phillip the Fourth.'"

A heavy silence settled over the deck, broken only by the rhythmic crash of waves against the hull. The revelation hung in the air — a cruel twist of fate, a bitter irony that turned their triumph to ash. They had found what they were searching for, but the cost — devastating, soul-crushing — left behind a hollow ache that reverberated through the vast, indifferent sea.

Jack pulled Breanna into his arms, her sobs shaking them both, a raw expression of the grief they shared. They had reached the end of the journey, uncovered the truth buried beneath centuries — and yet, the victory felt hollow. They had gotten everything they wanted... but the price had been far too high.

ST. AUGUSTINE

Bring Me That Horizon

Six months had passed since that night.
The late afternoon sun poured over the streets of St. Augustine in a warm, golden wash, the kind of light that seemed to bless everything it touched. A thunderous wave of applause rose from the crowd gathered around the City Hall steps, stretching across the ancient cobblestones like a living tide. Jack, Breanna, Greg, and the crew stood proudly beneath the fluttering banners, their faces glowing with victory. Hector stood beside them, his arm draped affectionately around a beautiful Latina woman whose smile mirrored the brilliance of the afternoon.

The Mayor stepped aside with a broad grin, and Tom moved confidently to the podium. The applause softened into a reverent hush.
"Thank you, Mister Mayor," Tom began, his voice firm and resonant. "Once again, we want to express our deepest gratitude to LaPointe Research and the Sandoval family for their extraordinary generosity in donating this historically significant find—a treasure dating back to the very origins of St. Augustine. And for their ten-million-dollar endowment to support the preservation of our city's most cherished landmarks. This legacy will live on for generations."
A fresh roar of cheers erupted, echoing off the old stone façades.
Inside the Castillo de San Marcos, nestled behind velvet ropes, a newly constructed glass display

shimmered in the filtered sunlight. Within it sat the ship's bell, the ancient gold cross, and the delicate letter from Carlos, now preserved for all to see. Together, the artifacts stood as a powerful testament to discovery, resilience, and sacrifice.

Back at the podium, Tom's voice swelled with satisfaction. "Thank you all for being here to witness this remarkable moment in our city's history."

As the ceremony concluded, the square dissolved into warm chatter and scattered applause. Tom turned toward Jack, his eyes shining.

"You did good today, son," he said. "Exceeded expectations."

Jack smiled, pride lighting his face. "Dad loved this place. We all agreed—it was the right thing to do. Ten million to the city, and a fair reward for the crew and the Sandovals. Besides," he added with a grin, "even Chip won't be able to spend all of his share."

"We'll see," Chip muttered nearby, but the spark in his eyes made it clear he intended to try.

Breanna waved goodbye as Tom walked off into the crowd. The crew clustered around Hector, laughter and joy swelling among them like music. Jack turned, only to find a reporter stepping directly into his path, microphone raised and camera crew in tow.

"Dr. LaPointe," she said brightly, "*The Extinction Protocol* drew spectacular ratings and has reignited the global climate debate. How does it feel to be at the center of something so impactful?"

Jack glanced at Breanna, her hand slipping into his. "We're proud," he said simply. "Dad was passionate about sounding the alarm, long before the world was ready to listen. I think he'd be thrilled that we didn't just fulfill his vision—we surpassed it in ways even he couldn't have imagined."

The two walked down the steps together, the crowd parting for them like a tide. Behind them, Chip and the others followed, basking in the glow of victory. Near the sidewalk, a man stepped out from the fringes of the crowd.

"Bonjour, Jack," Raymond said, extending a hand.

Jack barely looked at it.

"My condolences," Raymond added. "I considered Will a friend."

Breanna arched an eyebrow but said nothing, her eyes flicking between the two men. Jack's expression didn't change.

"What are you doing here, Ray?"

Raymond hesitated. "I was hoping we could discuss... reestablishing a working relationship."

Jack folded his arms. Breanna stood firm beside him.

"In light of all that's happened," Raymond continued awkwardly, "our board has embraced a new direction. We've approved a more ambitious, environmentally responsible initiative. We'd even like to propose a sequel—something that highlights our efforts to reduce our carbon footprint. A full corporate overhaul."

Jack and Breanna exchanged a look. Their grin bloomed slowly—satisfied, knowing, unbothered.

"A change of heart?" Jack said, his voice cool. "Looks like Big Oil finally saw the light. After we forced your hand, I might add."

Raymond flinched. "Yes," he admitted, barely above a whisper.

Jack gave him a long, level look, then smiled.

It wasn't kind.

"Goodbye, Ray."

He turned, and together he and Breanna walked away.

Behind them, Bobbi's voice rang out like a whipcrack.

"Too late, chump!"

Chip followed, tossing over his shoulder, "Yeah, take a hike, Frenchie."

Raymond stood frozen, his former arrogance drained away, left alone in the wake of their triumph.

Bobbi and Sam weaved through the dispersing crowd and caught up with Jack near the edge of the square. Bobbi grabbed his arm, her grip firm and teasing.

"Hey, Cap," she beamed. "We just wanted to let you know—we're off to Hawaii next month. A proper vacation. Finally."

She hugged Breanna tightly, and Jack laughed, the kind of laugh that crinkled the corners of his eyes. He shook Sam's hand with a firm grip, and for a moment, they all stood there—no longer survivors, no longer seekers—but victors, basking in the golden light of everything they had fought to preserve.

"You saved my tail more than once," Jack said, his voice thick with emotion. "I'm going to miss you guys."

"Me too, mate," Sam replied, clapping Jack's shoulder with a familiar warmth. The camaraderie between them was unspoken, years deep and hard-earned.

Jack turned to Bobbi, emotion cresting just behind

his eyes. "Three best years of my life," he murmured, drawing her into a long, heartfelt hug. "Enjoy the islands. You've earned every bit of paradise."

They continued down the street, their laughter trailing behind like a ribbon in the breeze. Greg walked ahead, radiating joy as he held the Latina close, his arm wrapped proudly around her waist. Hector's laughter carried through the air—bold, unrestrained—as he swept her into a kiss that made no secret of their growing passion.

Breanna bumped her fist lightly against Jack's arm in a playful jab, her grin wide with affection. The celebration still lingered in the air like electricity, their steps light, their hearts full. As they reached Jack's Jeep, gleaming in the sun like a trophy from another life, he paused and turned toward her with a glint in his eye.

"Hey, I've got something for you," he said, reaching into the back seat.

He pulled out a vinyl record. The cover read *SECOND CHANCES – JACK LAPOINTE*, with a photograph of Jack and his guitar, bathed in soft lighting and quiet confidence. Breanna's eyes widened, a gasp catching in her throat.

"You've been sneaking off to a recording studio?" she asked, laughing, her voice laced with surprise and delight.

Jack suddenly looked unsure, nervously fiddling with the edge of the album cover. He glanced at Chip, who gave him an encouraging nod, eyebrows raised knowingly.

"Do you mind?" Jack asked softly.

Chip shrugged, smiling. "Nah, I'm good."

Jack turned back to Breanna, his nerves evident

now. "I've been thinking about the right time…" He
hesitated, searching her face. "What I mean is—"
But Breanna had already slipped her hand into her
jacket pocket.
Her fingers trembled slightly as she pulled out a
small ring box. She held it out without a word, the
anticipation in her eyes sharp and beautiful. Jack's
breath hitched as he opened it to reveal a dazzling
diamond ring, its brilliance catching the late sun.
For a beat, he was stunned silent.
Then she held up her left hand.
A matching ring already adorned her finger, catching
the light with the same sparkle that danced in her
eyes. "What are you waiting for?" she asked, her
voice low, full of love, her smile wide with a playful
challenge.
Jack's laughter broke through, the sound light and
disbelieving. He slid the ring onto her finger, their
hands trembling together. And then he kissed her—
deep, certain, filled with everything they'd endured
and everything they had yet to begin.
Around them, their friends erupted in applause and
cheers. The golden light washed over them like a
benediction, warm and bright, casting long shadows
on the cobblestones. It was the kind of afternoon
that wrapped itself around memory, the kind that
stayed.
Still holding Breanna's hand, Jack turned to face the
others. "So that's it?" Chip asked, a gleam in his eyes.
"What's our next move?"
Jack grinned, a spark of mischief flickering to life. "It's a
big ocean out there," he said, Jack's voice buoyed by
everything he'd gained—and everything he was willing
to risk again. "You just never know."